A.T. Wright is a young and ambitious author who has a deep passion and love for fantasy adventure and the art of writing. He started his career as an author when at the age of thirteen he wrote his first novel, *The Legends of Ace Ford: The Northern Travels*.

In dedication to my parents and sister, who supported me through and through the creation of my book. Without them, Ace, Libbie, Jim, Becky and Austin would not exist, and for that, I give them my love and thanks.

A.T. Wright

THE LEGENDS OF ACE FORD: THE NORTHERN TRAVELS

AUSTIN MACAULEY PUBLISHERS™

LONDON · CAMBRIDGE · NEW YORK · SHARJAH

A CIP catalogue record for this title is available from the British Library.

ISBN 9781035830817 (Paperback)
ISBN 9781035830824 (ePub e-book)

www.austinmacauley.com

First Published 2024
Austin Macauley Publishers Ltd®
1 Canada Square
Canary Wharf
London
E14 5AA

In thanks to Austin Macauley Publishers, the company that brought my writing to life.

Chapter 1

Thunder shook the sky as bolts of lightning hit the ground with such unimaginable force. Rain whirled around the ancient city with snow meeting it. A storm and a blizzard had hit the old city at the same time, causing mass panic and destruction. Yet, the Obsidian temple still stood, with its black marble pillars holding up its cracked stone roof.

A beacon of pure energy erupted from the centre of the temple like a volcano spewing out its lava, with the clouds funnelling around it. Inside the temple, a man in bone-white robes stood, with his hood drawn as to hide his face. "He was meant to be here by now," whispered the hooded man.

That moment, a man in black robes and black animal furs strode to meet the man. He had a long, shaggy black beard and long, curly black hair; he had shadows under his eyes, and his eyes were blood red. His hands were thin and pale, and he wore black leather boots. At his side hung a large zweihänder sword; it had a crevice running down the blade and a black leather grip.

Walking at his feet were two hyenas, each with dagger-like teeth and red eyes like their master. "Greetings, Alex," said the bearded man. "It is good that we get to talk again."

"I wish that I could say the same, after you enslaved half my people," said Alex.

"I did what was necessary," was the reply.

Alex lowered his hood to reveal a blond-haired head, with brown eyes and perfect teeth. "I simply come to bargain, Lord Vex."

"Speak of your words, young one," replied Lord Vex. "First of all, if you free all my people, I shall offer my services as a servant, not a slave. Next, if you call off your army, I shall give you 700,000 gold. Finally, if you end your empire, I will end mine as well." Lord Vex studied the prince of the kingdom with great interest, yet Alex still stood his ground.

"May I say that this is a very generous offer, Prince Alex of Rimoor, yet I will not accept this offer."

"And why is that?"

"Well, for one reason, I am not ready to sacrifice everything that I have built up, Prince Alex," and with one swift move, Lord Vex unsheathed his blade and sliced a large cut across Alex's torso. Alex bent over and fell on the floor, the blood staining his robes and creating a pool of crimson blood on the floor. Alex coughed, which created a stream of blood coming out of his mouth.

"How could you?" Alex cried through retching and gasps for air. Lord Vex sheathed his blade and watched Alex bleed.

"Now I would let you die, however *I* am feeling generous today and will let you live. GUARDS!" Just after, four guards approached Lord Vex and the near dead body of Alex. "Guards, I would like you to take Alex here to the infirmary to have his chest stitched. Afterwards, take him to the island prison of Zanor. He will not be treated kindly there."

"Yes, my lord," replied the guards in unison. Lord Vex stood up as the guards lifted up Alex and took him away to the infirmary. He strode away, past the meeting room and private rooms (the private rooms being for the army and guards, of course) and into a dark room with a velvet carpet and a stone throne, which had a spire upon it that touched the ceiling.

Lord Vex sat down upon his throne as six guards in purple armour entered the room from side entrances. They then stood in even lines of three on either side of the throne. "Soon the kingdom of Rimoor shall fall and its people shall bow to the Exelon empire." Laughed Emperor Vex.

I awoke with a start. Oh yeah. Hi, my name is Ace Ford.

I'm a fourteen year old boy and this is my story. So where was I? Oh yes. I awoke with a start, my heart beating really fast, threatening to explode. I breathed in deeply and breathed out. "Hey, Ace. Oh, did you have another bad dream?"

"Yes, Jim. Thanks for asking."

"No problem, cause that's what family is for." Oh, and if you are wondering, no, Jim is not my actual family. See, I live in an orphanage and we just call all the other kids family.

"You coming down now cause I've heard that we are having pancakes for breakfast."

"Err, not yet, Jim. I just have to do my morning breathing exercises."

"Okay then." Then Jim went downstairs. Now just so you know, I am roommates with Jim and another guy called Austin, and I also have asthma so that's why I do breathing exercises (by the way, an inhaler does not help either.) After my breathing exercises, I got dressed and went downstairs. I went into the dining room, which was all brightly coloured with long tables, with boys and girls of all ages sitting upon benches that lined the tables.

Many adults were running around serving food, helping children and fussing over messes. I sat down next to my friends, Libbie and Jim, and opposite Austin and Becky. "Took you long enough to get down here," complained Austin.

"Well, I can't help it if I sleep in, can I, Austin?" Austin stared at his lap in defeat.

"Cheer up," said Becky, hitting Austin on the shoulder. "After panca..." At that moment, many carers walked in passing pancakes with syrup and cream to all the orphans except for the ones who hated them.

Well then. Hats off to the chef.

"Who said that?" I asked.

"Nobody spoke, Ace. Just enjoy your pancakes." So I ignored the voice in my head and ate my pancakes. After breakfast, we were allowed to leave the orphanage and go out into the city of San Diego. It being summer vacation, everyone was leaving and going to the beach or the pool, or even their friends who had parents. Me and my friends, we only had each other. "I know where we could go," said Libbie.

"Where?"

"The beach." My friends and I discussed it and agreed we would go there after pancakes. And that we did. After pancakes, we all got up and left the orphanage. Unlike the interior, the outside was just a brick house, a bit like a prison. We walked along the street to a junction, turned left while talking about which beach to go to.

"How about that new beach near the Brickston hotel?" Austin said. We all agreed on that location and went there.

Once we got there, it was full of people, all near the water as it was a boiling hot day. Me and my pals went down the beach looking at the sea and having a conversation about why so many people were on one side of the beach while nobody was on the other side. After a while of walking, we decided that it was a great idea to sit down.

We walked up to a rock and sat down on it. It was a freakishly warm rock. "Why is this rock so hot?" I asked.

"Errr, why would we know," replied Becky. Then the rock started to tremor.

"What's that?" Jim shouted. We all jumped off the rock and watched as not a rock emerged but a metal creature. And that was why the rock was so warm, because it was metal. The entire shape was humanoid but three times as large as your average human and made entirely of grey metal. The monster had no head, instead there sat a metal cone with no eyes, nose, mouth or ears visible.

It made a horrible metallic moaning sound as it thrust its arms up and threw them down, attempting to crush us. We all jumped out of the machine's way.

"WHAT IS THAT THING?" Libbie shouted as the beast attempted for another life threatening swipe. The monstrous creature opened up its right hand and out of the sand flew a giant metal sword. The blade flew into the monster's grip, it was nothing special, just a surfboard size sword with a very sharp edge.

"And now it has a sword," I said with obvious annoyance. The beast grabbed the hilt with both hands and sliced the sword through the air, attempting to cut us in half. Then the beast did another one of those awful moans and swung the blade down upon the floor. "There is something on its back," cried one of my friends who I could not classify at the time.

"Yes, I see it!" I said.

"Alright, I have a plan. All of you distract it so I can reach that weird thing on its back," and my friends gladly obliged. They ran around the metal monster, calling it names that I will not repeat. The monster, occupied with trying to kill my friends, left me alone. "Okay, I can do this," I whispered to myself.

I ran towards the beast when its back was turned to me and I jumped with all my strength to the weird thing sticking out of a crack in its back. I grabbed the thing's leather hilt and noticed that it was a sword. "Take your time, hon!" Austin shouted. The knock of the insult brought me back to reality. I pushed the blade deeper into the thing's back until a boom pushed me and the sword out and off the creature.

When I sat up, I heard a creak then the metallic monster falling forwards onto the sand. I walked to meet my friends at the front of the beast and noticed that the cone head had been blown off during the event of the boom. Out of the decapitated (deconed?) body crawled a starved man wearing nothing more than a dusty toga. The man cried and moaned as he escaped the body. "Thank you! Thank you!" He cried.

"Err, the pleasure is all ours," Becky said.

"Do you know how long I have been trapped inside that creature for? Six months," moaned the man. "Six miserable painful mon…"

He was cut off at the end of his sentence as his body started to disintegrate into red sand until all that was left behind was a pile of sand and a piece of blue metal. The piece of metal blasted into life as a small holographic video of a black haired man.

"Hello, Earthlings. My name is Lord Vex and I am the emperor of the Exelon empire. Now you have just beat one of my many golems. Oh yes. I trap slaves in the metallic body and use their life force to power my golem warriors. Now the prophecy states that people like you will leave your realm and enter mine to end my empire and kill my empire's god, Lord Sulleth."

"Apparently, if I try to delay the inevitable, I will only hasten it. So I still hasten it. Either way, you just killed one of my slaves and destroyed my golem, so now whether all of you like it or not, you are now part of a death prophecy, so good luck." Then the message shut off.

"Errr, what just happened?"

"I don't know but I have a feeling that we just got mixed up in something that we don't want to get stuck in." Even with the red sand pile and the body of the golem laying there, everyone on the beach still looked perfectly fine and undisturbed. Then the world spun under my feet. "Is this happening to you as well?" I asked my friends.

"Yes!" They all replied. Once the world beneath our feet turned purple and looked like a whirlpool, we fell straight into it, free falling into the unknown.

Chapter 2

Okay then. So we fell, screamed, fell, been sick a few times, fell; have I already said fell? I saw hundreds of shades of purple and green as we fell through the vortex of mystery. My friends (yes, I am not afraid to say it) and I screamed as well. Then after so long of falling, the world started to have colour again. Then to ruin that moment, I turned, so I faced upwards at the blueing sky.

Suddenly, I felt a shock of cold that went up to my chest as I blacked out and travelled into a dream. I awoke in a bright white chamber with great oak doors and as the back wall, a giant window, that took up all of the wall. Surrounding the walls were cased weapons, precious jewels and stones. But only two things caught my gaze, an eroded, scrap metal sword hung on the wall and, in the centre of the room, there was a cased, disembodied, corpse's hand.

The disgusting body part was green with many scars and gashes spread across it. Kneeling in front of the cased hand was Lord Vex, the mysterious man in the holographic projection.

"My lord, the prophesied ones have arrived on the furthest outskirts of Rimoor." Then a voice echoed around the room.

"*In a matter of time as well, they were taking too long anyway.*" It was as if it spoke everywhere, not just in one place. Then I noticed that it was the same voice that I had imagined earlier while eating pancakes.

"My lord, I start to wonder whose side you are on."

"*You should not question me, Vex.*"

"Sir, you are just a hand, you could not afford to lose me at this desperate hour."

"*Be patient, Vex, soon it will all make sense.*" Then the voice shut off and the room warmed by an incredible amount. Lord Vex stood and walked away from the hand and exited the room via the great oak doors.

Warmth spread through me as I sat in front of a crackling fire. I was in a fur covered room. I looked outside the window and noticed that it was snowing and it was dark out, which made no sense as it was summer.

"He is awake," said an unfamiliar voice.

"Great!" Libbie cried. I sat up on a large leather couch.

"Greetings, I am Cal. You must be Ace. I am the person that saved you by pulling you out of the snow."

"That makes…wait, thank you for saving us and hello to you. That makes no sense, it is summer."

"Oh yes, it is summer, but a few months ago, the Exelon empire came and set up camp in the Capital Land of this kingdom of Rimoor. They used the blizzard stone to cause a permanent blizzard across all of this kingdom; then storms permanently started the closer you got to the Capital Land. I live on the outskirts of this kingdom."

"So, we are in a different dimension, where we are part of a prophecy?"

"Yes, according to the message that your friends told me about," said Cal. At that moment, I looked around and saw my friends, all in new clothes and wrapped up in blankets with a hot drink in their hands. Then I noticed that I was wearing new clothes.

"How did I get into these new clothes?" I asked.

"Magic," replied Cal simply, as if it was the most obvious thing in the world. Austin gave me a look like *Just go along with it.*

"I see that you have Rince's blade."

"Whose?" I asked.

"Don't worry, Cal, I got this all covered. So Rince is pretty much the goddess of this land." Of course, being an atheist, I didn't believe in what Becky was saying.

"I will go off and bring in some pie for you guys and get you a cup of coffee, Ace," said Cal as he shuffled off into the kitchen. Surprisingly, the cabin was very spacious with many different rooms. When we thought that Cal was out of earshot, me and my friends started talking. "So there is a goddess called Rince and I have got her sword?"

"Yes."

"So there has to be some sort of devil, hasn't there?" Cal returned with a coffee which he passed to me and a plate of cottage pie for everyone.

"I will have this conversation with you," said Cal. "So Rince is the goddess of creation, the sun, life, and summer. She is also the goddess of many other things, however that is not the point of the story. So there was peace for centuries in this kingdom of many species, until the Exelon cult came. A group of fighters who disturbed the peace of this once calm kingdom."

"They followed a man called Lord Sulleth, the founder of the Exelon cult. They pillaged towns and kidnapped many; they fought many battles and won them all. Until one night, when the best warriors of the Rimoor empire had enough of the slaughter. They crept into the cult's camp and started a battle, and with the blessing of Rince, they won it."

"They killed Sulleth and chopped his hand off; they burnt the body and gave the disembodied hand back to the cult. It is said that they went into hiding and worshipped the hand as a god. We grew to think of Sulleth as a god ourselves, a God of pain, suffering, death and much much more."

"Wow!" was all I could manage. All of my friends gaped at Cal.

"So in the end, the fallen cult started an empire ruled by Lord Vex. It is an old folk story that Sulleth's spirit talks to Vex and gives him orders. Many people believe that the hand of Sulleth, which the empire still keeps and bows down to as a god, is alive with the spirit of Sulleth inside it."

"What about this sword? What is the story behind that?"

"Well, it is a legend that the sword was the blessing of Rince which led us to victory. It is said that the sword picks a host, in which it makes a spiritual bond with, so its wielder can control its magic capabilities."

I lifted the golden sword and said, "Hi, sword. Are we friends?" All my friends burst into laughter as I put the sword down.

"Well, it is getting late so you can stay here for the night. Pleasure to meet you all," finished our host.

"Okay, Cal, and thanks for everything you have given us," Jim said.

Chapter 3

When someone says *time to go to bed*, what you usually do is stay up. So that's exactly what we did. Once we heard Cal walk into a different room and start to snore (which he did very quickly), we all sat up on the sofas on which we were laying.

"No, I refuse to believe that we are in a brand new world with a weird goddess and a corpse's hand," I said.

"Well, start believing because this is one hundred percent real," replied Libby.

It was incredibly, no, unimaginably hard to compute. Like, what would you act like if you realised that you were in a magic land where it snows in summer and that you have to wander to the main land in a kingdom to stop an entire empire. No, just no. I looked out of the window out of a lack of words. I imagined walking up to that dark temple in the middle of a storm and a blizzard and saying to this so-called Lord Vex that he should bug off.

"Just stay calm," Austin whispered under his breath. It felt kind of sweet to be cared for by my friends, yet Austin was probably just talking to himself.

"Okay, I am going to sleep now," I said. Then I laid down and closed my eyes. Unfortunately, I did not have a dreamless night's sleep. I appeared on a ledge that overlooked a flat, empty, giant cave.

Next to me stood, the one and only, Lord Vex. He was just as I remembered, his red eyes and his black robes and furs. His leather boots and long, shaggy hair and beard. He had his hands behind his back with his hyenas prowling at his feet.

"Good. So very good." Vex laughed quietly. In the large cave below me, there were warriors. But these warriors had zombie bodies. Some parts of them were bone, some were flesh and skin, some were just organs, and some were just bone dust. Each of them wore either new shiny armour with sharp, shiny swords, while some wore eroding armour with eroded and jagged blades.

Many of these warriors were dragging people wearing cloths who looked like they were being starved. I guessed that they were slaves like the one we saved from the golem warrior. And, yes, you guessed it, there were many golem warriors spread out among the floor of the cave with their chests opened up to reveal a space just large enough to stuff a person within them. Like a cocoon.

Some of the slaves were screaming while others were crying, and others just looked blankly at the cave's roof, just waiting for the obvious. The warriors dragged the slaves in front of the open golems and threw them inside. With a snap, the chests of the golems closed up and trapped the poor slaves within the metal cone headed beasts.

This was the thing that made me furious. As I looked at those innocents being trapped, I felt an urge to save them and to destroy the empire's entire production. Behind dream me and Vex, a metal door slid open and a man in a metal tuxedo walked in.

"Lord Vex, some of the relic room guards have told me that they must see you immediately."

"You are dismissed." Then Vex walked off and exited the room while the door slid shut again behind him. I awoke in sweat and, yet again, new clothes. I looked outside and saw that it was daylight with very light snow falling. Around me, the room was empty with blankets and furs lying on the sofas.

"Come on, sleepy head, it's breakfast time," said Becky. I got out of the covers and walked with Becky to a marble table with comfortable looking seats surrounding it. In some of the seats were my friends, Libbie, Austin and Jim. I took a seat next to Austin and Becky sat next to Libbie.

"Okay. This is getting to a weird phase," said Libbie. Just when I was about to reply, Cal entered the room with silver platters in his hands and (you are not going to believe me when I say this) some platters floating around him, following him where he went. Cal had a big smile on his face.

"It has been so long since I have had the chance to serve other people other than myself," cried Cal. Then the platters zoomed off and positioned themselves on the table while Cal leisurely passed out empty plates as if nothing weird had happened. After the plates were set down and the platters full of food were set, Cal took a seat at the head of the table.

"Dig in then. I have not slaved over in the kitchen for nothing," Cal said. He said the last part sarcastically. My friends dug in first, and when I say first, I mean a second before me. I grabbed bacon, eggs, sausages and pancakes. I took a load of beans and tomatoes. Also I retrieved a glass and filled it up with (I hope it was) milk. I dug in.

"So, where is your sword?" Cal asked. At first, I thought he was talking to one of my friends, then I remembered that I was the one with the sword.

"I, errr, don't know," I declared.

"Come on," Cal said. "Check that new bracelet you got." I looked down at my arm and saw a bracelet, even though I was not wearing one the night before and didn't put one on that morning.

"How did I get this on?" I asked, looking around at my friends and Cal for answers. Again, I looked down upon the bracelet, it was completely golden but did not feel like a thing. It had no beginning and end, it was just a ring trapped on my wrist. Then I noticed glowing blue scribblings cut across it that were not there a moment before.

"There is something."

"What?" everyone asked.

Then I replied, saying, "It says, *Yes, we are friends, Ace.*"

"Reply it," Cal urged.

"So, err, what do you mean?" Then more scribing appeared, while the others faded. "It says, *You asked me last night, aren't I correct?*"

"Oh my," Jim said, "Remember, you did ask the sword if you were friends last night." Then the memory came back to me.

"Are you the sword of the goddess known as Rince?" I asked. Instead of more words being inscribed into it, the words faded and it spoke.

"Yes, I am Chorus. The almighty weapon of Rince. Sent down to this kingdom of Rimoor to protect those who could not protect themselves." All my friends gaped at my bracelet while Cal applauded with way to much enthusiasm.

"Ace, Chorus has chosen you as its host, the spiritual bond has been made."

"Okay, okay. Then, Chorus, why are you a bracelet not a sword?"

"Well," my bracelet replied. "I have the magical ability to change a form so I will be easier to travel with."

"Can you show me?" I asked. I didn't need an answer to that question. My arm instantly thrust itself upwards from under the table while the gold melted off my wrist and swam up my hand. Then, once the molten gold reached my palm, the thick liquid grew longer in my hand and grew heavier. A few moments later, I was not wearing a bracelet but holding a leather-hilted golden blade. It was nearly as long as my arm and was weightless.

"Okay," I said, starting to worry that all this weird stuff was not good for my health.

"Are you happy now?" The no-longer-bracelet-but-a-sword asked.

Just then, I noticed that Chorus had a weird type of voice (and no, it is not because it was a sword; well, maybe it was). It changed from between a definite male's to a definite female's. "Errr, why do you have a voice like that?" I asked out of inquisitiveness.

"Well, I will explain. See, I was made from gold, Rince's blood, and the blood of a male mortal."

"I still don't get it."

"Well, the gold gives me my form as that is my eternal form, yet the blood of a goddess makes me female while the blood of the male makes me, well, male. The best of both as you could say."

"Bravo!" Cal cried. Then Chorus melted and reformed back in bracelet form. After a while of chatter, we had finished our breakfast of discovery. Then Becky went off to get a bath while me and Jim talked about our situation. Austin was talking with Libbie, while Jim had a sorrowful look on his face. Jim had always had a crush on Libbie and he hated it when one of the other friends talked to her without him hearing.

Only me and Jim knew as one day Jim came up to me and asked if I could keep a secret, and when I said yes, he told me that he was, well, a secret admirer of Libbie. I also knew that Libbie had a crush on neither Jim or Austin, yet Austin did not have a crush on Libbie, he had a crush on Jim. Yeah, so what, I am friends with a gay person who has a crush on another person in the group. There is no problem with that, is there!

I could not tell anyone that Jim had a crush on Libbie, or that Austin was gay, because he made me promise not to tell anyone. Cal had told us that he was going into the kitchen to wash up. So it was just me and my friends in this weird wooden hut. It was still hard to compute. Stuck in a different dimension, check. Find out that you are a part of a death prophecy, check. Learn that you have a sword that is alive and has a spiritual bond with you, check.

And having to understand that you will have to adventure across an entire kingdom to a city where we will have to defeat not just an empire, but a god, a literal god, as well, not quite a check yet. Then Cal returned. "Okay, Cal, if we are going on a quest, could you, maybe help us like giving us a route," I said.

"Yes, let me just get a map." Then he ran off into another room and moments later, exited a completely different room with a rolled up piece of paper under his armpit. He went up to the dining table and unfolded the map. Me and my friends all gathered around the map.

"Okay," Cal said. "This is a map of the kingdom of Rimoor." He pointed to the bottom left hand corner. "This is where we are. At the corner of all of Rimoor."

"Okay and where are we gonna be heading to?" I asked.

"Here, the Capital Land," he said, pointing to the middle of the map. I gaped at how far we had to travel. Becky came out of the bathroom fully dried and in new clothes and walked up to us. "Travel plan I guess."

"Exactly," Libbie replied.

"So we just have to walk diagonally to the centre, right?" Jim asked. Then Austin looked at Jim with a dreamy look in his eyes that was like *Oh my god. You are an absolute genius.*

"No. Not quite," Cal said. "Okay, so the land in between this place and the Capital Land is festooned with undead warriors."

"WHAT!" My friends shouted.

"I can explain," I said, then I jumped into explaining the vision I had the night before. Afterwards, all my friends gaped at me for a moment or two before I said, "Carry on." Then Cal continued explaining.

"So, you will have to travel upwards to the top left hand corner of the map. Then you will have to travel diagonally downwards across the Grey Mountains then sail across the Goblin's sea."

"Why is it called that?"

"What?"

26

"The Goblin's sea."

"Oh, because there are many pirates that sail that sea and most of them are goblins."

"Okay, please continue."

"Okay, so where were we, oh yes, so sail across the Goblin's sea, then you must enter the Capital Land where you must dodge a few towns then enter the empire's commanding city."

"How long will that take us?" I asked.

"Around about a few months, yet the blizzard gets more stronger, then a storm is added to the equation not long after. So about a year."

"A year!" Becky said.

"Yes, that is what I said…"

"What's wrong, Cal?" Jim asked.

"Get down. GET DOWN NOW!" Then we looked out of a window and saw four zombie warriors walking towards the house.

Chapter 4

We did as we were told and got down. "Hide," Cal whispered as the undead warriors knocked on the door. Cal then went to the door and opened it. "Good morning, my good undead chaps," Cal said in an incredibly convincing manner.

"Greetings, Cal Lawson. We regret to inform you that we are taking you away from your property," the corpse in the centre said in a hoarse voice, which would make sense since the zombie hadn't spoken in years.

"But why?" Cal asked.

"The empire has been disappointed with your cooperation with them," said another creature. "And we know that you are hiding the chosen ones in your household." I looked towards my friends and saw them gawking at the warriors. Many thoughts were travelling through my mind at one instant. For example, *How did they get here? How did they know we were here? Does Vex have visions as well?* It all felt fuzzy like you had sat up quickly after laying in a hot bath.

"I will not leave my property for any reason," Cal stated.

The skeleton one of the warriors frowned (can a skull frown?) at Cal. "It is either you hand the chosen ones over and stay in your premises or we take you and kill the chosen ones right here at this moment."

"I will not leave my property for any reason," Cal repeated.

"Fine then," one of the warriors said with a sigh. "You chose the hard way." Seconds later, two of the warriors grabbed Cal around the arms and dragged him out of the door into the still, cold, snow covered land of Rimoor. Cal screamed to let him go but the warriors just seemed to ignore him.

"Come out, come out wherever you are!" One of the remaining two zombies said. They drew their shiny swords and searched the cabin.

"Okay, I have a plan," I whispered to my friends.

"I hope it isn't like the one that got us here," replied Becky.

"Haha. Now listen, Libbie and Jim, you run left. Becky and Austin, you run right." Jim had an ecstatic look in his eyes, probably thinking, *This is awesome, I am paired with Libbie*. While Austin had a deep look of disappointment on his face, probably thinking, *I am paired with Becky, great. I would prefer to be with Jim.*

"Okay! Three! Two! One!" I mouthed. Becky and Austin ran left while Libbie and Jim ran right. I looked at my bracelet and whispered, "Okay, time to shine." I willed the bracelet to turn into a sword as I leapt over the couch behind which me and my friends had hidden and, as I momentarily flew through the air, I found a golden blade with a leather grip in my hands.

When I landed from my action movie worthy leap, I charged one of the warriors who was distracted by Libbie and Jim running around him and sliced my blade through the chest of the creature, then I turned and beheaded the second. "Congratulations," said Chorus with its peculiar voice. "You have killed your first two enemies, but I forgot to tell you something about undead warriors."

"What?" I urged. Then I heard a clattering and scraping sound. I looked towards the zombies and saw their bodies reattach to each other, the rotten flesh of the upper body of the first (yet again) killed zombie moulded together with its lower half, meanwhile, the decapitated zombie stood up again and put its head back on.

"About that," Chorus finished.

"So, how do we kill these things?" I asked my sword (which was a sentence I thought I would never say).

"Easy, just do the exact same thing but with a burning sword."

"How do I do that?"

"Just will me to do it with your mind, harness my magical capabilities."

"Okay." Both of the warriors ran at me while swiping with their swords. I jumped out of the way and thought *fire.* When I looked at my sword again, it was blazing with a golden fire. The zombies turned and ran at me again. They just had enough time to look mortified with my blade as I chopped off both of their heads.

That time, they stayed dead. I thought the word *normal* and my sword stopped burning.

"Wow," Libbie said.

"Incredible," said Austin.

"Don't praise me yet," I said. "We must still save Cal." We ran outside and saw no such sight of Cal and the two zombies anywhere. However, the landscape was beautiful. There was a fence that surrounded the front of the cabin with a snow covered stone path leading to a gap in the fence.

Outside the fence was a large piece of land, all covered in ankle deep snow, hills and many other different pieces of land. Yet there was one thing the landscape had in common; it was all covered in snow.

There were a few pine trees to be spotted with, but again, snow specked on them. "How? Just how?" I said. "How have they got away so quickly?" I looked around at my friends' faces and saw that they must have been just as annoyed and infuriated as me. Cal had saved us from freezing, had given us food and shelter, and we couldn't save him from just four undead creatures.

"*Haha! You know what you must do, Ace.*" The voice in my head was talking to me again, and I knew that it must be the hand sized remains of Lord Sulleth, literally hand sized. Then my annoyance turned to pure hatred.

"*Yes, Ace! Yes!*" Sulleth cried as my vision started blurring and I passed out.

I saw Cal being dragged by the two zombies that kidnapped him through an ancient city. Thunder and lightning shook the city that I knew was the Capital Land. Even though a blizzard was raging with the storm, I saw zombies with their swords drawn, walking through the streets and slaying any stray wanderers of the city. Even then, I knew that even though a war was raging (and it looked ancient), it was still a city that was modern for whatever time we were in.

The Cal carrying warriors walked up to the huge, obsidian, Mayan pyramid looking temple. The beam of light producing from the temple's roof had not dimmed. They walked up to large wooden doors that led into the English Big Ben sized pyramid and pushed inwards. Waiting for them inside the temple was Lord Vex.

"Ahh, you brought him," he said.

"Yes, my lord," one of the two zombies replied.

"Great, continue with the procedure," Vex said as he pointed to a metal golem placed in the large hallway which they were in. "See, Cal is a traitor of the Exelon empire of the highest order, so I have had guards bring this golem out of the slave imprisonment cave under this temple so I can enjoy watching him being trapped in this golem warrior," said Vex.

The zombies dragged Cal up to the golem warrior, and I was forced to see him suffer the same fate as the rest of the slaves, to be trapped inside the golem.

Chapter 5

I awoke with a jolt.

"He is awake," said Becky.

"Vex did it," I said.

"Did what?"

"Vex trapped Cal in one of the golem warriors." My friends looked aghast as I explained to them my vision.

"So, what are we doing?" I asked.

"We are packing for the quest," Jim answered.

"Okay."

It didn't take a while. We just packed a few spare clothes, the map, and some weird gold things that had a large letter R printed on one side (which I supposed stood for Rimoor, the kingdom we were in) and a castle printed on the other. I took them thinking they were coins with a couple of bronze variants. We put on some fur coats and agreed it was time to go.

"So, which way is north?" I asked once we exited the gate. My friends gave me a look like *How are we supposed to know!* Then Chorus, my magic golden bracelet-sword buzzed on my wrist. I summoned it.

"About time. I have been in this kingdom for decades, why didn't you think that I would know which way was north," Chorus buzzed frustratedly in its strange mixed gender voice.

"Sorry," I said hoping that Chorus would still tell us the way north.

"Okay, look what's besides the cabin's walls," It said. We all did and saw huge walls of ice, as tall as skyscrapers, stretching further than the eye could see. Then my hand, which was holding Chorus, instantly pointed to the ice wall that went diagonally away from the right wall of the cabin.

"That way is north, just follow the ice wall away from the cabin. Well, if you did return to the cabin, then you would be back to the south-west corner of the map." I ran around to the back of the cabin and saw that the two ice walls met at a ninety degree angle (a corner if you didn't understand).

"The Exelon empire's blizzard stone created those walls all around the kingdom, shutting off its borders from the world so no help could get in and no citizens could get out."

"So we are literally in the corner of the map."

"Yes. Well, good luck," and with that final comment, Chorus shrank back down to the form of the golden bracelet. I went back to my friends.

"Okay, let's start walking."

For the first few hours all was good, but after that, it was starting to get cold and we were starting to get hungry and thirsty.

"I am sooo hungry!" Austin moaned.

"Well, we can't eat yet, we still have rations." Of course we couldn't fit all the food in our bags from the cabin (but we would have if we could have.) We found a few tins of food that said it was magically heated to never go cold. That got us excited as none of us knew how to cook.

It also meant that if we all decided it was time to eat, we just had to pull out plates, forks and knives, then open the tins and spill the food on the plates (have I already said that it was magically heated to never go cold. Stop pestering me, even though I can't hear you, and of course I am drooling right now).

I asked Chorus something through my mind, hoping it would work. "The days in Rimoor are thirty-two hours long, unlike your world's weird twenty-four hours," Chorus answered. After many more miles of walking, we decided it was time to settle down and pitch up our tent.

"So, how do we do this?" Jim asked. None of us had ever gone camping, well, you get the picture. We pulled out a cylinder, the shape of toilet paper.

"If this land is magic, maybe the tents are," Libbie suggested.

"Let's see." I rolled the cylinder onto the snow.

Nothing happened. Then the cylinder pulled itself apart and the bits took shapes. One bit set up a tent with five rooms, enough for all of us, already filled with sleeping bags and lockers. Another bit took the shape of a fire pit, already filled with wood, and it suddenly blazed into life. Two other bits morphed and changed to tree logs, long enough for two people to sit on, with more space to spare.

"Well, I think that answers our question," Becky said. We all picked rooms in the tent and brought out our plates, forks, and knives. We sat in front of the fire on the logs which had positioned themselves in front of the fire. We opened some of the magically warmed food and spilled some, not all, onto each of the five plates we brought and dug in.

The rest went by like a blur; we had finished our food and the plates instantly cleaned themselves, then we all went to our rooms. I zipped up the tent and entered my room. I laid down in my sleeping bag and closed my eyes. I wish that I had a dreamless sleep, but I was not so lucky.

I was in the relic room in the Exelon temple. No one was there except the cased hand of Sulleth and four guards. For guards that were meant to be protecting an evil god, they were not very impressive. First of all, they wore no armour, they were only wearing dust coloured robes. They had hoods drawn over their faces so I could only see shadows where their mouths would have been.

I had no clue how they could see with their hoods covering their eyes and noses. Yet the main thing that confused me was that they had no right hands. It must have been an insult to them as Sulleth's remains was a right hand, which his guards did not have. Now, I understand people can be born without body parts but it was just ridiculous, all of them having only a left hand.

"*Ace!*" Sulleth cried in his raspy voice like something sharp being cut through brittle metal.

"*Now we can have a chat in private.*"

"How about no." It seemed everyone else in the room couldn't hear mine and Sulleth's conversation. Every single word I said though felt like being stabbed in the throat.

"*You have a much bigger part of this prophecy than you realise, even more than your dear friends that you call family. Family! Disgusting thing. Me and you are not much different*

36

from each other, Ace. We are both people that have been abandoned by our families and are bitter because of that."

"I am nothing like you, Sulleth," I said.

"*Well, you better understand that our similarities shall help me more than you could imagine.*"

And with that, Sulleth let out a cold, hoarse laugh and I awoke in fear.

"Ace, wake up now!" Becky said.

"What? Why?"

"We are under attack!"

Chapter 6

I hurried out of my sleeping bag and summoned Chorus as I ran out of the already unzipped tent. My friends had armed themselves with harpes. You may be thinking, *why do your friends have harps as weapons?* Well, actually they are swords with a sharp sickle producing near the end of the weapon. We had found them in Cal's house and brought them in our bags just in case.

What I saw still haunts my dreams even to this day. The first wild monster I had ever fought. It was a wolf the size of an average car with the teeth set up of a king cobra. It had a mix of white and grey fur, for snow camouflage, and it was speckled in mud and dirt. Yet, the thing that scared me most was its tail; instead of a wolf's usual fur tail, it had a scorpion's tail and stinger.

"What the—" I started to say as the wolf spun around and sliced its tail at Becky. Becky parried the stinger with her harpe and ran backwards. Then it howled and turned towards me.

"Move, Ace!" Austin cried.

"I'm planning on," I replied. Then the wolf bounded at me with its snake teeth bared. I jumped out of the way and slashed the beast's pelt. It oozed blue blood, staining the snow that was below the creature.

"Yes!" I said.

"No!" Libbie said.

I didn't understand until I looked at the wolf again. Time seemed to go backwards as the blood floated out of the snow and back into the gash. The stained ground had turned back to normal white snow as the gash became a cut, then to wolf's skin and then was rapidly covered in fresh fur. I looked at my friends and saw that they were raising their swords again. I was starting to get annoyed that every beast me and my friends fought could not be killed.

"The maw," Chorus said.

"What about it?"

"It is its only weak spot. Just watch out for those poisonous fangs."

Then, I had a horribly ingenious idea, and I hoped Chorus would forgive me for my plan. The wolf turned on me again and let loose a loud roar.

"Sorry, Chorus," I said.

"Wait. What!"

Then I lobbed Chorus, point first, into the beast's maw. The monster only had a couple of seconds to look surprised as Chorus went down its throat. "What is happening inside the wolf's body?" Jim asked. Then suddenly, the monster doubled over and I saw something sharp flying around inside the beast's chest.

Return! I thought and Chorus cut through the beast's body and returned to my hand. I expected Chorus to be covered in blue blood but it was completely clean. From that wound the wolf didn't heal. A second later, the wolf had fallen.

"Well, that was fun," Jim said.

"Let's get back to bed," Libbie told us.

When I got back into my tent room, I was laying in my sleeping bag, looking at the ceiling, wondering if I would ever be able to look at a dog the same way again!

Luckily, the rest of my night was dreamless. When we were all ready to go, the tent automatically turned back into the metal cylinder without command. Libbie put the cylinder into her bag and we continued heading north, following the huge ice wall. The further we got north, even though it was already freezing, the temperature seemed to drop and the steady snowfall turned into a more rapid blizzard.

I couldn't imagine how snowy it would be in the Capital Land. But at least our luck made it so the inevitable storm hadn't been 'added to the equation' yet. I was wondering what would happen if I turned myself over to the Exelon empire. I hoped that the prophecy would not be about me and I would go back home.

"Guys," Austin said.

"What!" Libbie replied.

"The snow."

"What about it?"

"It's sand."

I looked down and noticed that the snow was golden. I looked for trees and they were all dead and leafless. "What's happening?" I wondered aloud. Soon enough, we came across a crystal blue lake with fresh tropical trees surrounding it. It would have been glorious, after so long in the snow, except there was a thing lying in the lake.

The water must have been shallow if the majority of the creature was still above water. I looked up and noticed it was a cloudless sky with a burning hot sun glaring down upon us. I turned around and saw that where the snow began, the sky became full of clouds, obscuring the sky, with snow falling rapidly. But as soon as it met the sand, the sky and land changed to the biome of a desert.

My friends retrieved their harpes from their bags and I summoned Chorus. We sneaked towards the creature. "Hello," I said. As soon as I said it, the creature rose out of the water.

"Hello, humansss," the creature hissed. Now, what the creature resembled most was Medusa from Greek mythology. The creature had a snake tail from the waist down, which was as long as a truck. But where the end of the tail was meant to be, was a viper's head, with eyes that were full of pale purple mist. From the upper body was that of a woman, but instead of skin, there were brown and pale green scales.

But the weirdest characteristic was the creature's head. It had a cobra's head, but where the face was meant to be was the face of a woman. She would have been beautiful if she didn't have snake teeth, a forked tongue and the same type of eyes that were full of a pale purple mist.

"Err, hi," Becky whispered.

"What brings you humans into my territory?" The snake woman asked.

"A quest," Libbie replied.

"Well then, welcome to my small, sandy home. I am Serpias."

"Well, hi, Serpias, I am Ace, this is Becky, this is Libbie, that is Austin, and he is Jim."

"What a pleasure to meet you all."

"Do you mind if we just pass through your land, we have to follow the ice wall."

"Sssorry, Ace. I can't let you do that."

"Why?"

"Because you are on my land, and I am now hungry." Then Serpias lunged at all of us.

Chapter 7

So we were in a cave. Serpias said that we needed to have a cave taste before she ate us, so she threw me and my friends into a cave and she slammed a huge boulder over the exit. "Well, this sucks," Libbie said, which I found quite an understatement. I looked around hoping to find a tunnel but all I found was a crevice in the wall.

"Austin, get here," I asked.

"What?"

"Can you fit in that crevice?"

"Of course you picked the smallest of the group." Then Austin got onto all fours and squeezed into the crevice.

Then suddenly, the crevice opened into a large tunnel.

Austin rose.

"Why me!" He whimpered.

We all marched down the tunnel and found, at the end, a crystal sitting in the pile of sand. Then I heard the boulder exit creak open.

"Time for dinner," hissed Serpias. Then she saw us around the crystal. Then I understood what I must do. I summoned Chorus and smashed the crystal. A blast of heat knocked me backwards. I got up quickly and ran out of the cave with my friends before Serpias shut the door on us.

"You destroyed the Desert stone," she wailed. Then the sand turned to snow and the rest of the land became what it would have been if it was affected in the blizzard. Serpias lunged and I dodged while slicing Chorus towards her. But the viper's head at the end of her tail whipped out and snatched Chorus out of my hand.

Serpias turned, baring her teeth, and Chorus whizzed back into my hand. With an idea, I hoped, I hoped with all my life that it would work, and I thought the word *pulse* and thrusted at the open air in front of me. A ringing sound in my ears began and Serpias was blasted back south.

"Hurry!" I said to my friends, wishing Chorus to return to its bracelet form. Then we ran. I didn't notice the blizzard getting stronger as we ran, I just thought about getting away from that snake woman.

After we finished running, I started my breathing exercises. "Are you actually kidding me!" Jim exclaimed.

"I know, now we have a Medusa creature chasing us."

As we carried on trekking, I fell behind to talk to Austin.

"Austin?"

"What?"

"I've been thinking, what would happen if we just…"

"Kill ourselves. Yeah, I have been having the same thoughts."

"But I know we can't."

"Why?" Austin asked.

"Because if we killed ourselves, the Exelon empire would continue growing and Cal would have saved us from freezing for nothing."

"But this isn't our world, we are just teenagers and we have been asked to do the impossible."

44

"But if we don't, this world will suffer, and I have a feeling Sulleth has something planned for our world," I said. "So if we don't finish this quest and prophecy, we would have just allowed an entire kingdom to fall at a corrupt empire's hand, so no, we can't kill ourselves. We will finish this quest even if we die trying!"

"That's a very inspiring speech," Libbie said, who had somehow stood right next to me while me and Austin were talking. "And that is why we think that if anyone should die, it should not be you."

"I'll just go," Austin said suspiciously.

"What's wrong with him?"

"Acceptance issues," Libbie said. "And I stand by what I said. Sulleth chose *you* for your little visions. Not me. Not Austin. You! Sulleth probably has plans for you, so if we have to, the rest of us will die for you."

"Errrm, thanks." Don't judge me. What am I supposed to say when your friend says *Oh, just so you know, I will die to save you and force the others to do the same.*

"See. The girl is smart. Perhaps she could be useful like you."

"Shut up!" I said aloud.

"Excuse me?"

"Nothing," I replied, but I knew that it was Sulleth tormenting me. But something got me wondering. What had happened in Sulleth's childhood that could drive someone insane enough to destroy such a peaceful place. Then I fell into the past.

Chapter 8

I was in a small house, surrounded by trees and farm fields. It reminded me of Cal's cabin, except this cabin was slightly smaller and near many other buildings that ranged from stone taverns (which I know was the case as there was a building made of stone that read 'The Stone Tavern') to wooden houses, huts, castles, temples, farm houses and a suspicious looking, half built pyramid made out of obsidian.

I knew I was in the Capital Land, but the Capital Land of the past; the Capital Land of when Sulleth was a child. Then the vision pushed me through the closed cabin door that stood in front of me, and I went right through it like I was made of gas. I saw an elderly woman in a straw rocking chair and an elderly man in a bed. I saw a middle aged woman running around a kitchen of wood and stone, making eggs and half cooked bacon.

"Sulivan," the woman shouted. "Please come down from your room and help your mother make your breakfast."

A young boy ran down from the stairs and hugged the woman that must have been his mother. "I'm here, Mother."

"Good, Sulivan, now could you get me the mixed herbs and sheep milk please."

"I can, Mother," and the boy ran outside. Nowadays, I realise that he didn't run to the fridge because fridges weren't around in this dimension. Back to mediaeval times. Minutes later, the boy named Sulivan re-entered with a metal jug of what must have been sheep milk and a wooden bowl of mixed herbs.

"I'm back."

"Well done, Sulivan." Then the scene changed. I was in a stone building with a wooden sign under the door that said, 'Rimoor Capital Land Orphanage'. "I don't wanna go, Grandpa!" Sulivan said.

"Me and your grandmother are old, we can't look after you. I know it has only been a week since your mother's death, but this is the best place for you now. You are only ten years old, I know, but you must hold on."

"I don't know if I can, Grandpa."

"You will do great things, Sulivan, great great things."

Then the surroundings changed again. I was in a gloomy stone room with few glass windows, full with straw beds. A group of people were kicking a twelve year old Sulivan. "You puny little wandought," a teenager laughed as he kicked Sulivan with his other friends.

"Please stop!" Sulivan cried.

It again changed, showing me Sulivan beating the kids that kicked him, except that this time, it was surrounded by mist, or smoke. The image zoomed out and I saw the orphanage in a blaze with many walls fallen. Many of the children and carers were burnt up and dead. Then Sulivan rose.

"Who is the wandought now!" He spat. Then it changed yet again to show an older Sulivan in armour with a large scimitar sword strapped to his side. He had long brown hair that fell to his waist and a small beard that was thicker at the sides than at the face. He had many warriors bowing at him and muttering while Sulivan looked down upon his followers with his arms outwards.

Then the army rose and they shouted in unison, 'All hail Lord Sulleth'. I didn't have to watch to know what happened next. I already knew what would happen. Sulivan being murdered by rebels of his cult, being burnt and his disembodied right hand being given back to his remaining followers, most of them slaughtered. Then I awoke.

I finally understood. The poor child Sulivan was Lord Sulleth.

Chapter 9

First, I noticed that I was in a bed. Then I noticed that I was in a tent. I got up and walked outside to see the gang sitting on a log, eating. "How long was I out?" I asked.

"Two days. It was horrible, we had to carry you!"

"Two days," I repeated. "Why is it so cold?"

Jim replied with, "Well, Cal said that it gets colder the further north we went, so now it is freezing, but luckily, the thunder storm hasn't arrived yet."

"Well, what did you dream about?" Becky asked.

"Err, what, nothing. I didn't have a dream."

"We know that you did, Ace."

Then I gave in. "Fine, I dreamt about Sulleth when he was alive and all the things he did." Of course I had to lie. I couldn't let my friends know that my life was familiar to Sulleth's. My life already sucked as it was. "How many miles did we travel while I was out?" I wondered aloud.

"Seventy-two miles," Chorus answered. "And soon Vex will send his most favoured human assassins after you."

"And how do you know that?" Libbie asked.

"Because I am part goddess. Oh, and by the way, another mile north is a small village, it would be a great place to stock up on some supplies."

"Chorus has a point, we have to get going," Austin said. It took us little time, as we had already packed up the campsite. Then we travelled further into the blizzard.

After twenty minutes, we arrived at the village. I honestly didn't understand what Chorus said about it being a 'small village'. It was huge! It had towering stone walls with a chain link gate the size of a lorry. We just passed through the gates which I found quite suspicious but, well, I was quite distracted as it was even more impressive on the inside.

It had small houses with blacksmiths and pubs dotted around the town. But it was no way near the size of the Capital Land that I had seen in my vision, so Chorus did have a point about it being 'small'.

"Where to?" I asked.

"Well, how about me, Austin, Jim, and Becky all go to a blacksmith and have our swords sharpened, while you get us something to eat and drink in that pub over there," Libbie answered. So I headed off to the 'Glacier Tavern' and picked a seat around a five-seater table.

Almost immediately a glass appeared in front of me. It was a glass of beer. I took the drink and took a sip (You are now thinking 'That's naughty, you're underage', and you are right. However, beggars can't be choosers, and I wanted to get drunk). "Hello there, you must be lost," said a man in a snakeskin tunic, which gave me shivers down my back after our recent encounter with Serpias, a red velvet surcoat, lion furs and silver trousers.

He had purple eyes and straw coloured hair with jewellery covering his ears, neck, hands, and even diamond teeth in certain places. However, two things disturbed me about the man. He had a huge scar running down from his forehead, past his eye and it ended at the bottom of his neck, and the other thing was a diamond encrusted whip that was curled up and hung beside his waist.

"Errm, I'm not lost, I am just waiting for my friends," I said.

"Oh, well, I am Collin. I own this tavern and practically this town."

"Okay."

"Oh my, you don't want to be drinking that," he said, snatching the beer out of my hands. "You want this, it is a cherry flavoured wine, more alcoholic but better tasting." He pulled out a wine glass and gave me it while pouring the wine. "Try it," he urged.

I took a sip. "That is delicious, thank you," I said.

"So, what brings you here?" He asked.

"A quest." Automatically I wished I hadn't answered. I began blurting out mine and my friends' entire story.

Afterwards, he just nodded.

"Interesting."

"What is interesting?"

"Well, of course, I can't let you do that. The Exelon empire has paid me to bring you alive, never mind about your friends."

"I won't let you." I rose from the table and summoned Chorus.

"Tut, tut." He clicked his fingers and four people who looked like ninjas, with katanas at their sides and a bow and arrow slung across their backs appeared. And each of them had one of my friends with a flintlock pistol at their throats.

"Sit," Collin told me. I fell back into my chair and dropped Chorus.

"*Ouch*," Chorus said in my head.

"I'm sitting down. Down, down, down," I said with a high pitched tone.

"Ace, are you DRUNK?" Jim yelled at me.

"Of course he is, I gave him extra alcoholic wine with a hint of truth serum. He told me everything about your quest."

"Quest!" I yelled randomly.

The ninjas looked concerned at each other like, *Why are we kidnapping this guy?*

"You see, these people." He gestured towards the ninjas. "Are Lord Vex's assassins, and he has set a very high bounty on you, Ace Ford, so I hope I will get a little repayment for finding you." He looked at the assassins. The one with the flintlock at Becky's neck tossed a coin sack. Becky took advantage of this and knocked the gun out of the assassin's hand and threw an apple at me.

I know this will sound crazy but the apple made me feel better. I recalled Chorus into my hand, many tavern customers screamed and ran for the exit, and I threw Chorus at the assassins who were all hit backwards, freeing my friends.

"Nice move!" I called to Becky.

"I know. What would you do without me," she called back. My friends unsheathed their harpes and charged at the assassins. They all unsheathed their katanas and ran at me and my friends. One of them locked in combat with both Jim and Austin while two others fought against Libbie and Becky. Another charged at me.

When the assassin reached me, I ducked as the assassin swiped his katana above my head. I returned to my battle stance and slashed at my opponent, but he blocked my move with his sword. I moved back and ran in for a stab, but the assassin easily just jumped over my head. As I had my back to the assassin, the assassin had a perfect chance to strike me and kill me, but he just slashed at my legs.

I crumpled to the floor. I wished Chorus had such abilities as I thought *heal*. Then suddenly, I felt like I was never cut. I rose painlessly and turned towards the assassin, who had a look of disbelief in his face. I ran into attack but the assassin recovered quickly and blocked my strike. We forced our blades against each other, hoping to disarm the other.

I thought *electricity* and a pale blue ark ran up my blade and down the enemy's katana, and he was blasted backwards. I looked towards my friends. The assassins had recovered their flintlocks and held them in one hand and the katana in the other. One of them shot a bullet that just missed Austin's ear.

Austin staggered backwards as the assassin reached into a pouch and put a single bullet down the gun's barrel and pulled down a lever. I realised that the assassins had old day flintlocks which had only one bullet and needed reloading after every shot, so I chose to take advantage of it. Then I remembered Collin. I turned around to see him unhook the diamond encrusted whip that hung at his waist and unravel it.

"Bring it on fancy pants!" I shouted. I ran at Collin but he whipped his weapon around Chorus and tugged at his whip slightly, throwing Chorus out of my hand.

"Really, Ace!" He shouted. "Disarming is the easiest manoeuvre to accomplish with a combat whip." I called Chorus back to my hand, but Collin anticipated the move and knocked Chorus out of its direction, sending it flying into a table. I then again recalled Chorus. I stepped back, knowing that if I got too close, Collin would be able to choke me out, or worse…

"Clever," I told Collin. I ran in for a strike but Collin whipped my sword, I knocked it away. Collin grabbed the end of the whip and ran towards me and we locked in combat. He swiped at me with his shortened whip but I parried the move. I slashed towards him but he sidestepped easily.

Then I screamed and ran towards him. I pushed against him and knocked him into an inside pond. Hearing screams, I turned and thought *pulse*, knocking the assassins backwards. "Let's go," I told them. We ran off into the blizzard.

Chapter 10

After the town was no longer in sight, we slowed down to a walk as I returned Chorus to bracelet form and my friends sheathed their harpes.

"That guy is a bit crazy," Ausin decided.

"Yeah. But I have a nagging suspicion that he was not in control of himself," Libbie said.

"What do you mean?" I asked.

"Well, he was obviously human, wasn't he?"

"Yeah."

"But he had purple eyes."

"You think that Sulleth was controlling him?" Jim asked.

"No, the feeling just felt older, eviller, more powerful…"

"Let's just forget about it," I said. "Our main concern is the Exelon empire, not some crazy guy's eye colour."

"Okay," Libbie finalised.

Time was complicated in Rimoor, sometimes time seemed to go faster, or much slower. So I will just save you some pain and skip a few weeks.

We sat around the campfire, eating our magical rations.

As I stared into the flame, a voice spoke in my head.

"Oh, Ace, tut, tut. Soon you shall understand true suffering; pain that you shall always remember."

"Shut up!" I muttered.

"What was that?" Austin asked.

"Nothing, just have a nagging feeling that the assassins are close by." In between the time of the Collin incident and where we were then, there had been many more monster attacks. For example, there was the deer with the human legs, the eel that chased us on a frozen lake, a lion with a spider head, and of course, some skeleton warriors from the empire.

We had also encountered some golem warriors. Oh, the pain at the time about seeing Cal being thrown into a golem warrior. If Rince was around, why didn't she just fight Sulleth herself. "Rince cannot fight Sulleth," Chorus said in my head. "As Rince resembles life, Sulleth represents death, and since he became a god, well, they are equally powerful, and with the empire growing, so does Sulleth's power."

"So, errrm, any more visions, Ace?" Becky finally said. Everyone had been eating in silence. As the nature that we were in a different dimension seemed to sink in, it seemed harder to react, or even think for that matter. I hadn't told them about my vision of Sulleth's past yet, but the pressure finally got the better of me.

"Yes, I have been hiding it for weeks now!" I cried.

"What!" Jim said. "If we are to survive this place, we are going to have to be truthful!"

"I know, it's just, the vision scared me, and I wasn't ready to share it."

"Okay," he said.

So I told them about my vision about Sulleth's history, and even explained how he was similar to me. "Wow," Austin said. "Just wow."

"I realise that if you don't want me to be with you guys any more…"

"Of course not, you're the hero here," Becky reassured.

"Really?" I asked.

"Of course, you are the heart and soul of this team, even if you are like the evil god we are going to eventually face."

"Thanks you, gu—" My sentence was cut short when an arrow landed between my feet. I looked where the end of the shaft was pointing, and at the top of a snow covered hill stood four people in black, one of them with their bow drawn.

"The assassins," Libbie said. The assassin fired three more arrows, each narrowly missing each of us.

"There are five of us, with a godly sword, there are only four of them, we can take them," Austin said.

"Two things, they have had years long training while we only had a few weeks, and they have the high ground. They have both advantages," I said. My friends drew their harpes and I summoned Chorus. As the assassin fired more arrows, I cut them in half with Chorus' heightened sense ability. Then the arrows just stopped.

"Oh my god!" Jim said. I looked up to see a woman-like figure with snake-like features pick up the assassin with the bow and bite his head off.

"Serpias has caught up with us!" Libbie exclaimed. Sure enough, it was Serpias, and she ate one more assassin then ignored the other two. She focused on us and slithered towards my friends. I watched as the remaining two assassins ran away. Then I saw Serpias was just one hundred yards away, still not slowing.

I raised Chorus and Serpias extended her index finger talon to the size of a Damascus steel sword, which then snapped off her finger and she grabbed it before it fell to the ground. So Serpias also had a huge sword that was many times the size of my sword. When we clashed blades, I almost fell down (Jeese, snakewoman, I'm just a teenager, be a bit more careful).

"You dessstroyed my home!" She hissed. Her tail swiped my friends off their feet, and whenever they tried to get up, she would just knock them over again. It was just me between the evil snake and my friends. I slashed my blade and Serpias parried. As she had the larger sword, she had a larger advantage, but I pressed on.

She jabbed her blade at my chest, and I nearly was impaled, but I ran backwards out of her sword's reach. "Get back here now!" She screamed.

"You didn't say the magic word!" I said while slashing. I tried to muster the energy to pulse her backwards but I was already battered from the fighting. Then I saw the assassins over Serpias' shoulder. They were running right towards my friends. A new wave of energy overwhelmed me and I tried something different.

I thought *meteor.* For a moment, I lost hope, then I heard something; then I saw it. I had just enough time to see Serpias gape at the sky when a piece of rock the size of a biplane hit her. She just went a few hundred yards, and I knew she was alive because I heard her wailing when the meteor stopped. It must have been too heavy for her to lift.

The assassins must have been buried under the snow as I couldn't see them. Then, I fainted.

Luckily, it was a dreamless sleep. I awoke with my friends dragging me like the game banana. "Hi, guys," I said. They dropped me. It wasn't painful as I fell onto the soft snow.

"Err, what's with your angry faces?" I asked.

"Well," said Becky crossly Crossley. "It's not like we have been dragging you for days now, and your thrashing in your sleep didn't help either."

Thrashing? I was sure I hadn't dreamt in my sleep. Unless I was truly asleep, but Sulleth was trying to locate me. It was far-fetched but a possibility. "Sorry, guys."

"Fine," sighed Austin.

I looked around; it was a completely different landscape, with very few trees and no hills, but it was completely flat. "This place is weird," I said.

"I know. One moment, hills and trees everywhere, but now." She waved her hand around. "Completely flat."

I pushed my foot deeper into the snow. It was much thinner here, and when my foot hit the solid surface… "Guys, we're on a lake," I told them. We continued following the ice wall that was frozen in the middle of the great lake. It kept crossing my mind, what if there were monsters lurking under the ice that covered the water, or if the ice suddenly broke and one of us drowned.

After twenty minutes of tense silence, I summoned Chorus and asked it something. "Chorus, do you know if there are monsters in this lake?"

"How very inquisitive of you!" It exclaimed. "But if you must know, some sort of creature is said to be lurking here, mind you, an unnatural one. One that Lady Rince did not make."

As though responding to the voice of godly weapon, a deep groan echoed across the river. "Let's keep going." We continued our nervous trek.

I knew that if I stopped, I would be an easy target for the creature. I kept Chorus at hand just in case and told my friends to draw their harpes. Suddenly, I doubled over, dropping Chorus, unable to draw full breaths. My friends ran over. "No, no, not now," muttered one of them. I couldn't tell which one as my ears were now starting to muffle all sound.

My head went blurry. It hadn't happened at all in this realm. I hadn't even needed to do my exercises, but it was all being built up inside me like a balloon ready to pop. I was having a major asthma attack. I was choking. I felt a crushing feeling in my gut. I was dying. In one of the most painful ways possible. At least I would be with my parents again, I was thinking.

But what if I didn't see them and ended up in an afterlife in Rimoor. I could only hear a rushing sound, like a tap running while your head is underwater. I couldn't see anything except for a black void that never ended. Blinded and deaf. Choking and unable to control my own muscles. Then suddenly, I saw something, but it was not the frozen lake.

I saw Vex sitting on a throne. People in purple armour, three on each side, were staring at the person standing in front of the stone throne. Vex looked deep in interest. I couldn't hear what they were saying. Vex obviously was furious as he threw a knife at the person, stabbing the forehead, instantly killing the guy. The dead person was wearing blue samurai armour but she had an ancient Egyptian khopesh hung at her side, also in sky blue.

She wasn't wearing a helmet, which was tucked under her arm, now rolling away from her dead corpse. Vex was tutting and shouted something at the guards. They ran forward and collected the body, dragging it out of the room from the door opposite the throne. Then I woke up, being able to breathe.

Jim was just finishing CPR while Becky had her hands on my jaw and forehead, opening my mouth performing what was unmistakably the mouth version of CPR. Her curly red hair was tickling my face. My eyes darted to hers; she had beautiful eyes, hazel coloured with a hint of grey. Then she saw me and stood up. I looked into her slightly tanned face; it was fading from the time in the snowy realm. I stood up.

"Thanks for saving my life," I said to Becky and Jim.

There was an awkward silence. "It's okay, just make sure we don't have to do it again," Becky said. We continued our adventure north.

Chapter 11

The ice was unsettling. I could just about see the end of the lake by the time it was getting dark. "Should we set up camp?" I asked. They agreed and we set up the tent and fire. We were running low on food supplies, so we all shared one can.

"I wonder how far we are from the next town? We could buy some more food there," Austin said. Libbie looked up, looking quite disgruntled.

"What's wrong?" Jim asked, his crush on Libbie kicking in.

"Nothing, nothing." She then went to bed early and we didn't see her for the rest of the night.

"A bit suspicious."

"What is?" Jim asked.

"Well, she seemed fine until we got onto the lake. She was in pure shock when you went into your asthma attack, Ace." Jim was pondering.

"I'm honestly surprised that we haven't come across Vex's assassins again," Becky said.

I was tempted to summon Chorus, I could use some information on the next town. But I didn't want to attract that creepy monster in the depths below. I got up and, as though on cue, the ice broke. I fell in, with just enough time to catch my breath. It was pitch black, with the lake floor so far down, and the snow that caked the ice covered top. I heard the watered down screams of 'ACE! ACE!' up above.

I had taken too long, I wouldn't be able to find the hole that I had fallen through. I summoned Chorus, it casting a weak light in the dark depths. I willed it to give me breath. Suddenly, I had a new surge of oxygen inside of me. Even though I wasn't breathing, I could breathe. I span around in the water, swimming slightly deeper.

I heard a deep groan from down below and a brush of something large moving through the lake. Then, I saw it. Well, I didn't actually see it. I saw a large shadow, a blackness that seemed deeper than the pitch darkness around me. I willed Chorus to pull me up. I flew right out of the water, the ice mending itself after me.

I was soaked to the skin, and the blizzard that forced against me was making it no easier to warm up. My friends wrapped my arms around their shoulders and helped me towards the tent. I heard snores from Libbie in her tent room. They took me into mine and zipped mine up. I let my clothes dry against the little fire pit in my room while I went to sleep.

I had another vision. I saw a dark hallway where Vex was walking. He was talking to a woman in a crimson cocktail dress. She had no major defining details as she seemed dead. I knew she couldn't have been because she was breathing, but she was as pale as a dead person, with dry, weedy hair and pale blonde eyes. Yes, I said blonde eyes, this realm was crazy.

"My lord, you couldn't be suggesting we send some golem warriors on five children," said the woman.

"Ahh, you see, Veronica," said Vex, "these children could be the end of the Exelon empire. They are the ones from the death prophecy," Vex told the woman.

"You don't really believe in that stuff? Sure Rimoor is a land of magic and wonders. But prophecies? A prophecy that says children would end an empire this great. I find it incredulous."

"It is true, you see, they have the blessing of Rince."

"The legendary sword, it is called a legend for a reason," Veronica continued.

"You must be willing to understand that we must take extra precautions now, it, as I have said, is prophesied. We have more than a hundred of those machines, what would it be to use a few."

Veronica complained, saying, "We may have hundreds of the golems, but we have thousands of our undead warriors. Entire legions."

Vex looked a little frustrated. "Fine then." Veronica looked pleased with herself, making Vex change his mind. But then Vex continued, "However, as the emperor of the Exelon empire, I command you to prepare two golem warriors to find the children, or else I shall trap you in one and send you."

Veronica looked terrified as she scrambled away. Vex continued down a large corridor, entering a chamber shaped like a box, with no windows and chains hanging down from the ceiling, restraining a man in a metal vest in which trapped his arms to his side. "Simon. Are you now willing to tell me what you know?" Vex asked the restrained man who must have been Simon.

"N-no," he said through a rattly cough.

"Simon, tell me what you saw in the Glacier Tavern and I may not need to chop off your head!" Vex said.

Simon choked, "Collin, he didn't have his regular eyes, they were purple. It was creepy. Then your assassins entered the tavern."

"Collin had purple eyes, ehh."

"Yes, my lord."

"That is all I need to know right now," Vex said, sneering sinisterly. He then walked out of the room, closing the door, leaving behind the screams of Simon.

"YOU SAID YOU WERE GOING TO LET ME GO! YOU PROMISED!" He shouted, as Vex locked the door, leaving Simon in the dark.

When I woke up, I dressed in my dried clothes, unzipped the tent and went outside. The blizzard was still raging but it was less furious than the previous night. The sun was rising. I sat down on a log and thought about my dream. I thought back to the time in the town, with the first meeting of the assassins. Simon must have been one of the people in the pub.

Then I thought back to what Libbie had said about the eyes. Then I thought that only I had been in the presence of Sulleth, even if it was just in a vision, so the power was filtered down, so he could have been the one possessing Collin. I must have sat thinking about it for a while because suddenly, they had all come out of the tent.

When I saw Libbie, she seemed much happier, like she had accepted something. Her chocolate-coloured hair and green eyes. I decided not to be inquisitive, so I didn't ask her about the night before. My friends must have decided this as well because they weren't asking Libbie questions.

"Good morning," she said, "Let's get going, if we find a town, we can have breakfast there."

"Okay," Austin said. "Let's go."

After we packed up the tent, we started towards the end of the lake. After five minutes, I could just about make out the shape of hills and trees. The blizzard was picking up again though, obscuring the view of it. Just then, a sound that ruined the morning happened. Ice cracking. In front of us, the ice broke away and was washed under the water, as the monster broke through the surface. It was terrifying.

It was pale blue and was about fourteen metres long. Its enormous maw was lined with rows and rows of teeth, each as long as a fencing sword. It was definitely large enough to eat Serpias whole. Its eyes were yellow and were cat-like slits. No doubt it was a gigantic snake. I had read about an extinct snake in the regular world, I think it was called the titanoboa. The creature that was in front of me was definitely not extinct.

But the thing that differed it from the regular world was the fact that when its tail broke the surface, at the end was a glistening hand, with enormous fingers and sharp talons. As it slithered out of the lake, it turned around and headed straight back to it. Its head then dipped under and some of its body, the peculiar hand tail was still above water. Then its head and a small portion of the body that went under again surfaced.

It must love the coldness of the freezing lake water. Then it opened its maw. Through instinct, I summoned Chorus and heard my companions draw their harpes. Then Chorus suddenly jerked to the side, pulling me off the ground and tripping all of my friends. We skidded across the lake, Becky and Jim hitting their heads against the ice wall.

"Oww!" Jim complained. Standing up again, he looked at the snake and froze. And when I mean froze, I mean he froze. He was suddenly coated in rock, looking much like a well-made statue.

"It's a basilisk!" Chorus cried. "I had to. Look around but don't look in its eyes." I turned around swiftly to see a pink coloured goop lying on the ice where we were standing. It was burning through the ice.

"What the…" I started.

"Don't worry for now, Ace, I put a stupidity charm on the serpent. It's the only reason you guys are not dead yet. But the charm will break soon. Those things usually last five minutes but basilisks have strong minds."

"Okay, Chorus, tell me about it quickly."

"Alright, so by the looks of it, it is a baby—"

"A *baby!* It's huge! Are its parents down there?" I shouted.

"No, basilisks die after giving birth, and the fathers, they die after the mother, kind of like a bond. But yes, that basilisk is still a baby. So overview! Some say that if you look a basilisk in the eye, you die, but that's wrong. What really happens is that if you look them in the eye, you're okay, but in direct eye contact, you freeze and turn to stone, like a coma."

"How do I reverse it?"

"You must kill the basilisk that did it, that way the magic will die with it and they will unfreeze, as if out of a dream. Second, they spray poison goop. That pink stuff may take a while to burn through ice but it will melt a human in a second. Although, that one second will feel like a minute of sitting in an electric chair kept on high power."

"And those hands at the ends of their tales, they may seem like they couldn't do much with it, as it is at the end of a tail, but basilisks can use those hands like a skilled hand to hand warrior."

Suddenly, Chorus began to heat up so hot, I nearly dropped it. The charm had broken, the basilisk was loose. I wheeled around to see all of my friends frozen. "Damn!" I had to fight that thing all by myself, well, with Chorus.

Being stuck in a magic realm is not good for your sanity. Just going to leave it at that. I didn't know how I was going to fight the basilisk without looking at it. I just started looking at its mouth, and with each flinch of its head, I jerked my head down. I rose Chorus and held it with both hands. Then, faster than I thought possible, the basilisk's hand swiped at me.

I missed it by centimetres. I slashed my blade downwards, with Chorus being a magic blade, I thought it would cut through the snake. I was wrong. When the hand clenched like a fist, and brought it down to where I was, I cut through the air, and with a slip, I fell on the ice. I looked at the hand while scrambling to get back up. It wasn't even cut. But the smash had broken a new hole in the ice, slightly smaller than the other that was burnt by the acid.

The hand withdrew and the serpent opened its mouth. Through little holes in the side of its maw, it sprayed more of the pink goo. Thinking *shield*, I blocked the acid, however it all burnt a ring around me, sizzling further. Its mouth then opened vertically, and with its fangs, it brought its head down towards the ice in which I was stranded on.

I, using Chorus' power, pulled myself across, narrowly missing its maw and stumbling to a halt on the ice. The eyes, which I looked at, suddenly flicked towards my face. Noticing it a second early, I looked up and jumped, bringing my sword down on its face. It skidded across its scales and plunged into one of its eyes. The basilisk let out an awful cry and plunged underwater, face, hand and all.

I looked down at the ice. The blizzard was pushing me around more severely now, as if responding to the danger I was in, making it harder for me to stand my ground. I saw the dark body lurking under the frozen lake. Then it thrust upwards, bashing its head against the ice, splitting it, and sending me across the lake. I fell into one of the ice holes.

With it being a permanent winter, and it being a body of water, I felt paralysed. Then I thought of the word, *breathe*. I could breathe while holding my breath. Then I noticed the dark shadow of the basilisk swimming towards me through the pitch blackness. I pushed myself forwards with a small pulse behind me summoned by Chorus.

I pushed myself forward again, stabbing my blade into the basilisk. Well, it again just skidded across its scales but I felt a slight cut appear on it. Then the basilisk did something I was not expecting. It made a tight turn and swallowed me. Being swallowed by a snake, mad amounts of claustrophobia washed over me. It was like being crushed by ten lorries, except I hadn't died yet.

The magic of Chorus must have been protecting me. I couldn't move my arms and legs. I was like a board of wood. Then I thought *explosion.* The force of it blew the snake up from the inside. Covered in snake guts, I swam back up to one of the holes.

"Guys. Guys! I see Ace," cried Austin. They rushed to my side, almost running, and got to the edge of the lake.

"Sweet, sweet solid land," I said. The blizzard was pricking my skin now. I stood up, thought *clean*, and the serpent's innards disappeared. We walked, following the ice wall north. We came across a village an hour later. It was much smaller than the town where we met Collin and definitely smaller than the Capital Land where I was seeing in my visions.

Oh, and it was populated by elves. Let me tell you, the town was the most modern place I had seen yet in Rimoor. Even though there were only around twenty houses, each and every single one of them looked like a modern villa which you could find on Earth. Also, the town hall was incredible. It was four floors tall, and was pure marble. In fact, it even had windows made from diamond.

I know that you want to know about the elves, so I'll just say, they were *weird.* They were all unhealthily pale and all had dark grey eyes. They had vampire-like teeth and the same grey hair. The only way I could tell the difference between the male elves and the female elves was that the male ones wore fur trench coats, silver encrusted tunics and leather trousers, while the females wore white leather dresses.

Oh, and of course, they had the signature elf pointed ears. As we walked along a cobblestone road, we attracted some disgusted glances from the elves. We didn't see any cafes, restaurants or bars along the way, but we did run across the village square which had a few small huts. "This place is worrying," Austin said, as we headed towards the huts.

Even though the huts were the size of a broom cupboard, and had regular wooden doors and simple metal walls, we walked towards one, as it was so much different from the surrounding buildings. Then a strong gust of wind pushed

Austin to the floor; the snow had become so strong now that it had started to bury him. We hurried towards him and pulled him up.

"Close one, eh, could have lost you," Jim said. Austin blushed deeply, though it was hard to tell because of the cold. When we opened the door to one of the huts, we saw a marble staircase leading downwards. As we trekked down the stairs, the single file downwards corridor opened up slowly until torches burnt on braziers along the staircase wall where all five of us could walk down side by side.

Finally, we stepped off the staircase and saw something that could only have been made from magic (which it probably was). We were on the floor of an underground restaurant. Red carpet led down the vast chamber to a stage where someone was sitting on a platinum throne. We obviously noticed that we should not be on the stage.

The one on the throne was wearing a dress made from white leather, except that the lining of the dress was lined with white fox furs. She was wearing a platinum caesar crown with silver jewellery around her neck and wrists. We walked towards a table.

As we left the carpet, I noticed something different about the marble floors. It was heating through my boots.

"Magic!" I whispered.

We sat down at a table that seated five and food magically appeared in front of us. "I bet you Cal would get along with these creatures, could share some magic tips," Becky said.

At the name of Cal, everyone seemed saddened and depressed. Then a golden goblet of heated liquid appeared next to my meal. I took a sip. It was incredible. It was like a warmed sugar drink which had sweets sitting in them for an hour then taken out. I looked at my friends and saw them sipping the drink.

Then suddenly…

"Greetings all to Breden restaurant of Golden Woods village. Thou are all lucky today to have the mayor here with us." A new elf that was on the stage gestured proudly to the elf on the throne. "And I would like thou to lend thy ears to our great mayor." The elf moved off the stage as the mayor rose from her throne.

"They have a very posh accent." I heard Libbie giggle.

"Hello, my elven friends. As thy know, I am thou mayor," said the elf in a velvety voice. "I hope that thee are enjoying thou meals. News says that the Exelon empire has not yet found our village's location." Cheers went up from the elves enjoying their dinner.

"However, I have heard that humans have entered our town, locals have been reporting." Me and my friends sank deep into our chairs, trying to hide from view. "And if thou see them, report it to the local guards."

The elf sat back down on her throne and a magnificent feast table appeared out of the ground in front of her. A hearty feast appeared and she started to eat. Slowly, a murmur arose again until the entire chamber was full with chatter.

"Okay, after this meal and drink, we have to get out of this town," Libbie said.

"Agreed," Jim said.

We ate as quickly as we could without being suspicious. Finally, after what felt like hours, we had finished. We had risen and began to leave when the hood on my winter jacket fell. An elf on my left gasped and shouted, "HUMANS!

DISGUSTING HUMANS IN THE RESTAURANT!" All of the elves turned to see the humans that were us.

Suddenly, there were guards standing in front of us, all of them in silver armour with gold chainmail. "Humans, thy are coming with us," one of them said.

We walked back up the staircase, through the village until we reached the town hall. We entered through double polished oak doors and then led up a staircase. We turned and walked through many corridors until we came across double doors that were made from birch. They were intricately made, with patterns of huge thrones and elves hunting.

One of the guards knocked and a voice said, "Enter." Then we were pushed through the doors.

Chapter 12

There was a large corridor-like chamber which was completely black, unlike the other places in the village. It was windowless and had huge flames in bowls hanging from the walls. Four huge black and grey thrones were set up on either side of the wall, with what I guessed were elves sitting in them. The elves I saw on the thrones differed from all the other ones I had seen.

They were wearing black leather robes and diamond crowns. I couldn't see their body shape or their faces (which were hidden from the hoods on the robes). At the far end of the chamber sat a more elegant throne, made of platinum and gold. It was smaller but much wider. I was forced to stop on a cobblestone circle, which differed from the black concrete floors.

I looked around, the guards pushed my friends onto the circle as well. Then, from the doors where we had entered, the mayor walked through, walked down the room, passed through the circle and sat down on the throne at the end of the chamber. She made a waving gesture with her hand and one of the robed elves began to speak.

"Humans, thou have been taken here, in front of the elven council, because thee have trespassed into our village. Do thy object?"

"This is purely unfair. We simply just came to top up on supplies, have a meal, then leave. We have better places to be than here," Libbie said.

"Hmm. Thou are humans, thou probably work for the Exelon empire."

"No no, we are here to end the empire, we are on a quest," Libbie continued.

"Silence!" Another one of the eight council members said. "Thee are humans, and are on elven land, we have the right to strike you down here and now, yet we are waiting due to the fact that you may be enemies of the empire."

"I know what we do might seem quite suspicious, being humans on your land, but you must believe us, we are the only chance of ending the empire," I pleaded.

"Only chance, eh. What makes thee more capable of facing Lord Vex than ourselves? Us elves are masters of bow and arrow, sword, and dagger. And what are thy, mere human children," said a third.

"The prophesied ones," the mayor whispered.

"I beg your pardon, my lady," said one of the council elves to the mayor.

"They are the prophesied ones, the ones who were sent to Rimoor by magic. They are here to end the empire."

"Thou don't really believe these children, do thee?"

"I do, we must let them go," the mayor said urgently.

"I do not believe this!"

"So we can go?" Austin said.

"Yes," said the mayor.

"No!" One of the council members cried out. "This is preposterous, the council will not allow this. Mayor, thou shall be evicted from your throne immediately, and thee humans. All in favour of exterminating these ghastly beings."

"I!" All of the council cried.

The guards lowered their spears and advanced towards us. Then a huge boom echoed across the room as the door was blown off its hinges. Three golem warriors stomped in, each heaving a huge metal sword behind them.

"The Exelon empire has found the village! The humans have led them to us!" The council elves cried out.

I summoned Chorus and my friends unsheathed their harpes, while the guards ran across to protect the council members, who were all sitting in their thrones in horror. The machines advanced, me and my friends prepared for a big fight. It would be much harder with no weapon sticking out of the cone headed machine's back.

A feeling of dread surrounded me as I knew that any one of them could be Cal. They continued their approach, each of them lifting their swords into both hands. I ran forward and skidded under the legs of one. I turned around, seeing my friend's dispatch. I made a thrust towards one of the warriors, the sword skidding against the machine's metallic cover.

The golem roared. I knew that they were the cries of the poor slaves trapped inside. I conjured a blast of flame, the heat sinking into the monster's shell. Suddenly, I was up against the wall; the second of the three golem warriors had hit the flat of its blade against my ribs. Starting to stand up, a flaring pain pushed through my body. I thought *heal* and rose, the pain in my side gone.

I charged again, slicing at a greave in the metallic armour like shell. A small clump of metal fell from the mass. It let out a moan and brought down its blade. Narrowly missing, I jumped up and plunged my blade into the cone like head. Pushing the blade down, I removed the head off one of the warriors. Just before it collapsed down to the floor, I leapt onto the shoulders of another.

I repeated the process on the second one and it began to collapse. I jumped and landed onto the floor. Running to the third (and final) one, me and my friends gathered around it, all plunging our blades into a greave and running sideways. When we removed our swords, the third golem warrior collapsed. I looked around and saw three slaves escaping from their dead, robotic shells and running away.

Without looking back at the elven council and mayor, we escaped outside the town hall. Ghostly flames danced across the houses of the elves, with trees reduced to ashes and elven bodies lying lifeless. Screams roared. I shouted that we should leave and we escaped out of the town, running north, and not looking back.

We didn't stop running until we entered a dark forest. It was pitch black night time and the blizzard made it all the more terrifying.

"Should we get out of here and go around?" Becky asked.

"No, it would take too long, we have to go through," Jim said, speaking with confidence and authority.

We steadily walked through the slowly thickening forest floor. No doubt many vicious, predatory monsters lurked in the forest, but I forced myself not to think about such things, it would drive me mad. But what if I was just mad. In a coma where I believed I was in a magical dimension. However, the thought made no sense as I was knocked unconscious many times in Rimoor yet I always woke up in the snowy land.

Soon the trees thickened so much, we had to walk single file and a light patter of snow fell from the tightly woven branches. It seemed like midnight even if it was during the height of the day. The crunch of the snow below me was eerily satisfying, in a way that was not meant to be in a forest like this. After a few minutes of walking, I couldn't see my friends any more.

"Guys, where are you?" I asked. There was no reply.

I summoned Chorus and thought *light*. Suddenly, the huge tree trunks around me and the floor was visible. But I couldn't see my friends.

"Chorus, what is this place?"

"Why are we here?"

"We stumbled across it when we were escaping the elf village."

"No, no, no."

"What is it?" I asked.

"We are in the forest of imagination."

"But that sounds like a good thing."

"It would make you think so, yet imagination is the most dangerous weapon of all; it drives the strongest insane, it makes one see things that one is not meant to see," Chorus said. "This forest may not bring your worst fears into this world but it will make your worst fears haunt you. They awaken from the depths of your mind and when you see them…"

"We gotta get outta here."

Then I heard it. Then, I saw it. Myself. It was standing alone in front of me. It was a copy of myself, with the deep brown eyes and grey hair, even though I was only a teenager. The thin body was so much like my own. Except for one thing, it was alone. I don't mean that it was alone as in it was by itself (yet it was), I mean it was alone mentally.

I could see the loneliness of it and its depression. My worst fear. Being alone. I could feel my sanity slipping away. I ran and ordered Chorus to find my friends.

Chorus pulled me from the front and around the trees, over rocks and through clearings. All the while I could see the occasional flash of myself from behind the trees or in the open. But as soon as I saw them, they were gone, after every blink. Soon I came across Austin who was on his knees crying. I couldn't see what he was crying about, as it must be in his head.

I ran up to him and shook him by the shoulders. He didn't even twitch. I put Chorus in front of him and the light from it must have awoken him from his trance. He looked at my face, tears trickling down his face.

"Ace?"

"It's me. I'm going to get the others. Come on." I grabbed Austin by the wrist and dragged him along beside me as Chorus pulled me along. The next one I found was Becky. She was standing with her eyes open, with her hands clutching the sleeves of her winter coat. I shone Chorus in front of her. She broke out of her nightmare.

"Grab onto Austin's hand!"

Becky clutched on and off we were again. Next, I found Libbie. Her face was contorted in pain and was moaning. She was curled up on the floor in a ball. I again shone Chorus in front of her. She woke up. "Libbie, hold on." She clutched Becky's hand.

The nightmare version of me was flashing everywhere now. Then I found Jim. He seemed okay, except that he was sweating like mad. I shone Chorus in front of him.

"Ace, is that you?"

"Yes, hold onto Libbie's hand." Jim looked ecstatic all of a sudden. He grabbed on and we ran in a single file. Chorus guiding us. Then we were out of the forest. We all broke apart. The forest moaned as if it was calling for us. It was night time. We had been in the forest for hours. I sat down and fell asleep on the floor.

I luckily didn't have a vision. Unluckily, I had a nightmare. I was in the middle of a country road. I was running along the empty road, a dark force chasing me. I turned a corner and found the orphanage I lived in. I ran inside and along the corridors and up the stairs. Then, I was suddenly in a dark forest, with snow below me and myself flashing before me.

I ran out of the forest and found myself in the Capital Land. Snow and rain separately assaulting me in the dark. Then the force got me.

Chapter 13

I woke up in front of a fire. I looked around and saw my friends sitting around it on the logs in the magic campsite. I was laying in the snow.

"It was the only place you didn't stir. We tried the tent. You only stayed calm when you were in front of the fire on the floor," Libbie said. I stood up and sat down on a log, either side of Becky and Jim.

I didn't see the forest anywhere.

"Where's the forest?" I asked.

"It's right behind you, you just can't see it because of the blizzard."

I turned around and saw only snow crashing into the kingdom floor, the forest hidden. "We really should have gone around that place," I said.

"I know, that place, it was worrying; it was like I was lost from reality," Austin said.

An uncomfortable silence settled across me and the others, as I knew that they would be scarred much like me from the event.

"What did you see?" I asked. I knew it was a dumb question. Why would they feel comfortable sharing their deepest fears with me? But Becky told us, "I saw nothing. I couldn't see, I couldn't hear. I was isolated from the world. It was like someone had just turned off the lights in my mind."

"I was at my parents' funeral again, except it was an open casket and my parents' voices were calling me a failure in my mind." That made sense due to the fact that Austin was the only person that knew his parents and came to the orphanage as a young boy of eight.

"I was being bullied, kicked, hit, and stabbed," Libbie whispered. Again, this made sense as Libbie was assaulted by a gang of abusive children when she was ten at school. She had been stabbed and sent to the hospital. This had happened because some children were making fun of her because she didn't know her parents.

"I was being burnt alive in a fire, it was my worst fear come to life," Jim said.

"I had a vision of myself but I was alone. It seemed like me but I could see it in the dark echo's eyes, it was alone, abandoned and lonely," I told the others confusedly.

We sat in silence again, however, it was less uncomfortable, more like we had just told each other about our deepest fears (which we had) and were feeling calmer and more secure. Then I stood up and went back to the tent, as it was still night. I zipped up my tent room and went to sleep.

I woke up in the morning feeling like a million dollars. I went outside to find Jim and Becky already out there. As soon as I was out, I was closely followed by Libbie and Austin.

"Good night sleep I hope?" Becky said.

"Yes, and I didn't go into a vision, which is good," I replied. We all sat down on a log and ate some magic breakfast of dragon egg and howler meat (which I hope is not poisonous).

It was quite nice. "So, we better plan our quest a bit more carefully," Jim said.

"Why?" Libbie asked.

"Well, let's face it, we keep on running into trouble, first with Serpias then the assassins. Then the elven village which I think is destroyed."

"Fair enough," Austin said.

"So, we need a more thought out plan."

"Well, we can't really. This place is not like the city we have grown up in, this is a different dimension, and at that, I literally cannot see a few metres ahead because of the storm," I said.

"Okay, Ace, we'll use your strategy, just run blindly into danger and fight our way out."

"Yep," I replied. "It has worked so far, so let's keep on doing it."

"Okay, okay," Jim concluded.

We packed up the camp and prepared to set off. I had grown so used to woolly coats by now that I honestly didn't care if I slept in them. We walked around until we found the tower-sized ice wall (which was also obscured by the snow). We got into an open huddle and walked north.

We had been walking for a few minutes until I realised that I was the only one not talking. Austin and Libbie were in a heated conversation and Jim and Becky were talking about food. I started thinking about how long we had been travelling, and how much longer it would be until we went back home. I summoned Chorus.

"Greetings again, we haven't talked in a while. What has been bothering you, Ace?" Chorus chided.

"Nothing, I just wanted to know something," I said.

"Hmm?" Chorus pushed.

"Well, I was wondering how far we are until we reached the topmost corner of the kingdom."

"Good question. Let me think. So, if you are a while away from the forest…" It took Chorus a while to figure out the location, until it finally said, "You are approximately halfway to the north."

My mouth fell open. "What! We have been travelling for weeks, how are we about halfway!"

"Rimoor is a freakishly large kingdom, much like what you earthlings would call a country."

"So we are travelling across a country."

"Yes, pretty much."

It was appalling as we had travelled for god knows how many weeks. We were only halfway. "Are there any more towns on the way to the north?"

"Yes, one or two, it has been years, I am not too sure."

"How much longer would you say we have until we reach the north?"

"A few more weeks, the snow is disturbing my magic." Just a few more weeks, then we will be climbing mountains then sailing across a ring shaped sea to a city that makes Las Vegas look small. Marvellous, just marvellous. I morphed Chorus back to a gold bracelet and continued marching forward.

"Hey, Ace! Slow down, we nearly lost you," Jim shouted.

Without noticing, I had walked so far ahead of my friends. "Sorry!" I shouted as I jogged back. "I asked Chorus, we are nearly in the north, we just have to keep on going for a couple more weeks."

"At least it isn't months," Libbie said.

"Well, remember, we still have to get across the Grey Mountains then sail across the sea, so it still may take months."

"Don't make me think it may take that long. I already hate snow, I don't want to hate everything," Libbie said.

"Okay," I said. The walk was becoming more and more tiresome as the snow both tried to push us back and torture us as it murdered every bit of open skin available to them. But we made it work, that was until I saw a flash of black. I summoned Chorus. "Guys, get your swords!"

"Why?" Austin asked.

"The assassins are back."

My friends all unsheathed their harpes and gathered back to back, creating a protective circle, me among them. Then without thinking, I flicked my sword to the right. I looked down and saw an arrow cut in half laying on the floor. Did I really cut an arrow in half mid-air? Yes, yes, I did.

Then Chorus whispered, "You know that wasn't me, it's because our magical bond is becoming stronger, you can harness my magical capabilities more easily." I raised my sword. Then suddenly, my arm went overtime.

My sword arm was flashing so fast, it was like lightning, with each slash ending with two halves of an arrow on the floor. When the bombardment of arrows ended, I looked down to the floor again and saw so many arrows laying there. Then I heard a bang of a flintlock pistol and my arm instantly moved away and my non-sword arm (my left one) caught something.

I looked at what I caught. It was a singular, rather large flintlock bullet. I caught a *bullet!* I dropped it to the floor. I heard one of the assassins reach into something and pull out another bullet. Then I heard the sound of some hard powder (what I guess was gunpowder) falling into something (probably the gun) and the sound of someone sliding a piece of metal down a tube. Then I heard a click of someone pulling a lever. The assassin was reloading the gun.

"Get 'em!" I shouted.

We ran forward, creating an expanding circle. I raised Chorus and jumped. I landed on my feet with my sword pushing the assassin's katana to the ground. I then stepped backwards and released the katana. Just as the assassin was regaining his wits about what just happened, I was charging forward and jabbing towards my opponent's gut.

Chorus was then parried and hit out of my hands with two clever moves used by the assassin. I leapt sideways and grabbed Chorus from the snow. I rolled backwards and held Chorus with both hands. The assassin laughed as he sheathed his katana and drew his bow and arrows, so quickly it was nearly a blur. He fired multiple arrows towards me but with my new found skill, I ran towards him, cutting the arrows out of the air as fluently as water.

I then jumped forward, spinning around, creating a sort of sideways helicopter movement. The move was dodged as the assassin slid sideways on the snow. I heard the clash of swords and the occasional sound of a fired bullet, but my mind was concentrated on survival against the assassin. Quickly shouldering his bow and unsheathing his katana, the assassin was ready for melee combat. I ran forward towards the assassin and used my smaller size to my advantage.

I slid under the wide, arcing slice, in which the katana was carving and knocked the assassin's katana out of his hands. I kicked it away and pushed my sword under his chin. The assassin then slid something out of his sleeve and threw it to the floor. He fell onto his back and shuffled backwards. The thing that he dropped was a chunk of metal, which then blew up in a flash of orange light.

The smaller fragments of metal were still held together by an orange webby substance. Then out of the substance crawled five zombie warriors. The orange web was a gateway; it was how the Exelon empire forces could get around so quickly.

"How do we beat these things again?" I asked Chorus.

"You need fire," It replied.

I thought *fire* and Chorus' blade was suddenly aflame with a brilliant blaze. I looked at one of the zombies, four out of five of them were half eaten away corpses, wearing rusted armour and wielding rusted swords. The fifth was wearing brand new armour, polished and a gleaming sword, sharpened as well. They ran forward.

I saw the assassin running to retrieve the katana I kicked away but then my focus was shifted to the five enemies. I attacked one of them. My sword rose above my head, I brought it down. The other four were slicing and jabbing at me, I just had enough time to parry their attacks. I cut one of the lower rank ones (I guess the ones with nicer armour were higher rank) head off.

I then turned and jabbed inside a fleshier, human-like one. I pulled my sword down like a lever and pulled out the zombie's rib cage. Then with a wide arc, I cut two others down. Then I faced the final one, the one that I guessed was a higher rank. I saw a ferocious gleam in its one eye (the other side of his face being completely skeleton). I pushed my blade against it, then I pulled away.

Rushing forwards, I sliced at its sword. We were stuck in a contest for the offensive. At one moment, I was blocking and parrying attacks, the next I was slicing and jabbing, with the enemy blocking my attacks. Then I was able to push the zombie's sword above its head, and I cut its torso off from its upper body.

I faced the assassin, who was again charging. I then ducked and the assassin ran right into Chorus. My sword plunged deep into the enemy's gut. He went limp and I stood, allowing the assassin's dead body to fall. I ran towards Becky. When the assassin noticed Chorus still ablaze, and the assassin's corpse and five dead (can something dead die again?) zombie warriors, he pushed Becky's harpe away and ran.

I made fire Chorus extinguish and looked as the other assassins saw the other running and following suite. They must have realised that their ambush was not thought through enough. I looked at the weird portal web thing. I kicked one unanimated corpse at it and it fell through. I tried putting my foot through but it just pushed the web down, much like what would happen if you pushed your foot down against a plastic bag.

I kicked the dead assassin at it and it fell through. The web must have been magically designed to only allow forces of the Exelon empire through.

"Hey guys, are you alright?" I heard Jim shout.

"Yes," everyone shouted.

"Yep, I'm okay," I shouted back. Of course, I was still thinking of the assassins that had survived, and how easily the Exelon empire could reach me and my friends. However,

Chorus saying we were only a few weeks away from our destination was pushing me to continue.

"Which way is north?" I asked Chorus.

"To your left."

"Okay thanks." I ordered Chorus back into its bracelet form and I called my friends to come over. Once we were back on the move, I ran up to Austin.

"Hey."

"Hi," he mumbled in return.

"So, I have a plan. If we continue north and don't enter any other towns or villages, unless absolutely necessary, we should have an easier shot to reach the Grey Mountains. Also if we have watches at night, we can make sure no members of the Exelon empire can sneak up on us, including nature's creatures, and wake each other up at the crack of dawn."

"Why are you telling *me* this?" Austin asked.

"Because you were the only person walking alone," I said. "Which is quite unusual for you."

"It's just that since we got here, to this kingdom, we have been around each other twenty-four seven. I know! I know! We usually are either way but not in a situation like this!" He spread his arms outwards into a crucifix like manner. "Like it's still sinking into my mind that this is not a dream, and I just needed some time to think all of this through," Austin said.

"Do you want me to leave?" I asked.

"Nah, it's okay, Ace. I think I just needed to get that off my chest," he replied.

"So, what do you think of the plan?"

"It's good. But I think we have to put into consideration the possibility of Serpias still being alive."

"True."

"Should we tell the others about your plan?"

"Sure."

Then me and Austin turned our heads in front of us and saw a horrific scene...Jim had his tongue stuck to the ice wall to our left.

We ran towards Becky, Libbie and tongue-on-the-ice-wall Jim.

"What happened!" Austin shouted.

"Okay, so maybe me and Libbie dared Jim to lick the ice wall," Becky said.

"But why?" I asked.

"Well, Jim was always saying to us that he wanted to lick a huge ice cube. Well, when he told us, me and Becky began thinking, so we dared him to lick the ice wall 'cause that's practically a huge ice cube, right?" Libbie said.

"Yeah but just...just...just why?" I moaned. "We could have already trekked a small bit further north, into land that we cannot see or predict because of the blizzard, and you guys coincidentally decide to do that now when we are just a few weeks to the Grey Mountains, and not at the beginning of our quest when we could see what was actually in front of us."

"Christ, sorry, Ace. It was just a joke," Libbie said.

"I know it is, just we are nearly at the mountains, which I am nervous about because of my asthmatic condition and high altitudes will make it all the worse for me." Then it happened again. I began struggling to take deep breaths, my throat closing up and my chest constricting. I began eating air as I fell onto my knees. Closing my eyes, I thought about pancakes back at the orphanage, where, even if I was free from that place, I still missed.

I began gulping down larger breaths, fixing my breathing by using my breathing exercises. I opened my eyes and began to stand up, all the while doing my breathing exercises, and after about seven minutes, I was able to breathe again with ease. I then took a deep breath and said, "I'm fine."

My friends let out a long sigh. All of us remembered Jim and turned back to him. With his tongue still frozen to the ice wall, he mumbled, "Waaaal is making maa tongue berry, berry colb!" Which I guessed meant, 'Wall is making my tongue very, very cold'.

I summoned Chorus and pointed it at Jim's tongue. Jim let out an awful scream. "Shush, I'm not gonna hurt you," I said. I then pointed the tip of Chorus to the ice and thought *free*. Jim then fell backwards with his tongue free from being stuck. I summoned Chorus back into being a bracelet. "Feeling better?" I asked.

"Bess," Jim said. Which I again supposed he meant 'yes'.

"Are you gonna get up?" I asked.

"Oh bess," Jim said. He began to stand up when I heard something. It was the howling of humans…or zombies.

"Ok, let's get going," I said.

We began walking north again, zoning out of the howls. "ACE!" Libbie cried. I turned around to see Libbie walking towards me.

"Why did you shout my name?" I asked.

"Well, I was saying your name, you just didn't hear me."

"But how, it doesn't seem too windy?"

"Well, how far can you see in front of you?"

"Not very far, the blizzard is getting too strong."

"Exactly, I think the amount of snow is beginning to drain out all sound."

"Is that even possible?" I wondered.

"It seems so. But you have to think, we are in a magical realm where the laws of physics must vary."

"True."

"Well, Austin told me that you had a plan."

"Oh yeah."

So I told Libbie the plan. She seemed to be more observant of the plan and made some good suggestions. Once I finished telling her the plan, I asked her what she thought.

"I think it's a great plan, and the idea with the towns, that is very wise. We don't want any more people like that weirdo bar owner."

"Ahh yes, Collin."

"I'm still concerned though," Libbie said.

"Why?"

"Well, don't you think it's a possibility that Sulleth has already anticipated your plan, well since he is a god and you seem to have a connection with him."

"Yeah, the connection is starting to worry me more than before. Like, I think I might see something that will interfere with our quest. What if I see more things that could stop me from wanting to complete the quest?"

"*More things?*"

"Well, the fact that we are the ones that got trapped here and have to liberate a country-sized kingdom, it makes me want to crawl up into a ball in the corner of the snow and go to sleep, and just hope that when I wake up, it would all have just been a dream."

"I understand. All of this is just messy, but we gotta consider that this IS reality and us five, we gotta set all these people free. Think about the animals here that were made into puppets for the empire, think about all the elves and innocent citizens of this land whose lives could quite easily have been ruined by the empire. Consider the brutal and selfish kidnapping of Cal just so he could give us a chance to save his home."

"Thanks...I needed that," I said.

"It's completely okay 'cause that's what friends are for right."

"Right."

Then I looked up and noticed that it was night. "How quickly does the sun set here?" I wondered aloud.

Then Chorus spoke in my head saying, "It roughly takes ten minutes for the sun to set in Rimoor."

Then the other guys came running up to us.

"Wanna test out your night time strategy?" Becky asked.

"Yeah sure," I said. We walked for another five minutes to flatter ground (we had just been going up and down a few hills). "Here's good," I said.

Becky pulled out the metal toilet roll and chucked it on the floor. It suddenly expanded into the campsite.

"Still amazes me," I whispered.

"What? How the tent works?" Jim asked.

"The tent, the swords, the entirety of this kingdom's magic. The magic here is just unimaginable," I replied.

"I'll take the first watch," said Jim.

Then came a bombardment of 'Oh, it's okay, I can do it' and 'Are you sure' and 'Okay'. Of course I was one of those people who said 'Oh it's okay, I can do it'. After Jim quietened everyone down enough for him to be heard, he said, "No, I will do it. My tongue is still frozen, I won't be able to get to sleep with it. It's just the smarter move."

"Okay, if that's what you want," Austin said. All of us then climbed into the tent, except for Jim, and went to our rooms. I then heard my friends begin to snore as I drifted off to sleep, without any of us having any food.

I dreamt of sunlight (understandable since I hadn't seen sunlight in weeks) and huge beaches on a hot day. People on the beach relaxing and having a great time.

"*You miss your homeworld. I know you do, Ace, I can see it in your mind*," Sulleth's voice said. As usual, if I ever heard him, it was always in my mind yet seemed to emit from the air surrounding me.

"*Hot beaches. Warm weather. Makes me loathe even more the heat that is Rimoor's natural climate. Of course I need the cold climate for my empire so the soldiers can survive*."

"GO AWAY!" I shouted.

"*HA! Your pain amuses me. Humans I never understood*," said Sulleth.

"Even though you once were one," I countered.

"*Once. Even though I am bound in my disembodied hand, I am still the most powerful than I have ever been. And I still have plans for you*." Then the voice shut off. The beach around me changed. I was standing in the middle of the Capital Land, the rain and snow whirling around me. The funnel beam emitting from the temple still blasting out with full force.

I let out an awful scream. Then I woke up.

94

Chapter 14

I was in my sleeping bag in the tent. I went through my breathing exercises, stood up, and went outside. Sure enough, Jim was asleep against the tent wall. I grabbed him from under his shoulders and heaved him into the tent, into his room and onto his sleeping bag. I left the tent again, zipped up the entrance, and took the place against the tent where Jim was. I decided I would take the rest of the night in the position of watch.

The snow was still blasting down with full force, obscuring the land in all directions. Even the ice wall was faintly visible. Pine and fir trees were still dotted around, even within my small area of view. I pulled my winter coat tighter around me and started rubbing my hands together. "Ever so cold tonight," I whispered to myself.

I heard the light laughter of Sulleth emitting from the air surrounding me. I began thinking yet again of the vision of Sulleth's past. It still shook me how such a young, sweet boy named Sulivan could end up secretly ruling an entire kingdom. Another fact that constantly rang inside my head about the vision was the fact that the main temple headquarters of the Exelon empire was already in construction before the creation of even the Exelon cult.

It made me think that ever so possibly that the temple was being constructed as a temple for the Rimoor goddess, Rince, but became desecrated during the rise of the empire as they took complete control over the kingdom. Then I heard a loud hiss and was violently reminded of Serpias, and the fact that she was more than likely still alive and tracking me and my friends down.

I jumped up after I heard a loud laugh. It was not that of Sulleth but more so of something that existed in our realm, but couldn't just place my finger on it. Realising that even though it was an animal, it might be simply a small monster snail with a rock for a back that could laugh really loud. *Of course it isn't a snail, Ace!* I thought to myself.

I summoned Chorus and crept lightly towards the origins of the laugh. A few moments later, I turned around, just to see myself blind from the ice wall and the campsite. All I could see was swirling snow and a few trees. I kept calm and continued towards the origin of the laugh. Another laugh echoed, louder now, seemingly closer.

I raised Chorus in two hands and whispered to it, "Do you recognise that noise?"

It replied saying, "Yes, and no."

"What do you mean yes and no?"

"I mean I haven't heard that creature for years but I still remember it. It is some sort of giant cat."

"Cat?" I asked.

"Well yes, a creature you would call a monster in your land but what us beings from Rimoor call simply 'animals'."

"Can you explain?" I asked urgently, yet still quietly.

"Yes. So the animal has the head of a hyena, its where it makes its hunting call, the laugh. It has a huge bobcat body, perfectly coloured for both night and day hunting. It has a tail of roughly fifteen feet. Oh, and it is also one of the fastest Rimoor animals alive."

"Great, of course I had to get into this," I complained near silently.

Another laugh echoed, yet again closer. A rustle behind me triggered a natural instinct to turn, a mistake I wish I could have taken back. I saw a huge furry tail gliding through the trees. Looking at the way the tail was moving, I saw a huge cat's body, the head and parts of the body shrouded within the shadows. Another laugh produced from the direction where I was looking. Sure enough, the monster I was looking at was the laughing Rimoor animal.

I attempted to tread carefully away from the creature, yet with my luck, my second footstep backwards let out the world's largest snow footstep crunch. All of my other footsteps on snow crunches were average in loudness but obviously now had to be the time I stood on an unlucky patch of snow. The animal's movement stopped for a moment, as if contemplating its next move, then it stopped circling around me and launched itself straight towards me.

I jumped straight to the right, narrowly missing the animal's large claws. I rolled over in the snow, slowly rising again. Once I reached my feet, the animal was already jumping at me. This time, I was more prepared and rolled under the beast just before it landed on the space I was just standing on. I rolled onto my feet and I stood up with such fluidity, it seemed like I had practised that dodge for years.

I turned rapidly to see the animal skidding along in the just above ankle deep snow. Once the creature had stopped its skid, it began to turn at full speed, and of course, since the existence of the physics of speed (which seems to exist in the realm I was in) meant that the animal had to make an enormous turn to reach the position of charging at me. Realising that the animal had only two speeds, full speed or sneaky prowl, I decided to use it as my advantage.

As the monster neared me, I sidestepped and held Chorus out. The monster noticed my sword and jumped over it. I turned yet again. The animal had turned to its prowl and turned towards me. Then I noticed that its tail was dug into the snow…BAM! I was pulled off my feet and fell onto my back. The animal had hidden its tail in the snow behind me and pulled a move which hauled me off my feet from behind.

I made a left-way roll and stood up to see the animal already aware of me rolling. It began to run towards me again. Dazed from the move, I was unprepared, so just by pure luck I survived. The animal slipped on a harder patch of snow and it rolled away from me. Gaining sense, I realised the creature was already running again towards me.

As it closed in on me, I jumped away at the wrong time. The hyena head's opened maw closed in around my right foot, and because of the animal's motion, the monster simply broke my leg. I looked towards the animal which was slowly prowling towards me. I began to shuffle backwards, although I was too slow to get away.

I eventually slumped on the ground and stared as the animal reached me. Its head glared down at me, its mouth opening, drool dripping within the mouth. One last laugh escaped the monster's mouth. Just as it pushed its head towards me, aiming for the face, likely attempting to bite my head off, I raised my sword and thought one word.

Looking back now, I really think that some epic music should have played as an electric blast came out of Chorus and, well, blew the hyena's head up. I thought the word *Heal* and my leg suddenly snapped back into place. Then I passed out. I began to think that the entirety of the quest mainly revolved around my friends carrying me about. Luckily, it was dreamless.

I began to faze into consciousness, feeling incredibly cold. Light surrounded me, yet it might as well still have been night because of the fact that my vision was blurred. I closed my eyes and opened them again to find myself in a different area. My blurred vision cleared and I slowly began to stand up. Once I had stood up, I thought the word *Chorus* and my blade flew out of snow and into my hand.

A fresh patch of snow had settled, yet the blizzard was still in full effect. Indeed, it was day, but I was lost. I looked around to see nothing.

"Where is the camp?" I asked Chorus.

My sword replied saying, "Turn around, no, not that far, further…wrong way. STOP! Go straight forward and you will reach the ice wall."

I began to walk forward. It took roughly five, maybe six minutes to reach the campsite. I saw my friends anxiously sitting on the logs around the fire.

"Hi!" I shouted towards them.

They turned towards me, then they stood up and ran to my location.

"Where *were* you?" Becky demanded.

"Yeah! We were terrified, we were afraid the empire had got to you!" Austin said.

"Okay, okay. So I went outside and heard a laugh. I activated Chorus and went to check out the sound." I then told my friends the rest of the story. The expressions on the others weren't as extravagant as I would have imagined, which is understandable as we had previously seen a wolf-scorpion and even a snake woman.

"Okay, thanks for telling us," Becky said. We then continued to pack up the tent (after having breakfast) and prepare for our day's endeavours.

Chorus then began to talk to me within my head. I began to think of words, which were, "*Hi, can you understand me this way?*"

Chorus' reply was, "*Yes.*"

"*So, can you tell if any enemies are near us?*" I yet again asked.

"*There are no Exelon forces as far as I am aware, yet there are few animals.*"

"*Any more of those animals we killed last night?*"

"*No,*" Chorus replied.

"*Do you think our…erm…magical bond is growing,*" I wondered.

"*Yes, you seemed to more easily use my abilities last night.*"

"*That's good. Are there any other abilities that may be useful?*"

"*I cannot say, you must discover my powers for yourself.*"

I looked around and saw Becky and Jim in deep conversation, while Ausin and Libbie were pleasantly strolling along in silence. I wasn't sure if I wanted to start a conversation at the moment, so I also stayed silent. While silent, I took in the scenery. It was the first time I actually took time to watch the Rimoor landscape.

Even though I was enjoying the occasional tree and fresh smell you never got in the city, I still felt depressed. A thought echoed within my mind, that Sulleth said something about Rimoor being quite a warm kingdom. It made me wonder how many people had died during the rise of the empire. So many lives lost simply for a dead person to have more power. It was despicable.

"So, Libbie, what do you think about the quest so far?" I asked.

"Well, of course it is scary knowing we are in a place that we have no intellect over. Also the thought that we are nowhere near halfway done is also unsettling," she said.

"That's true. I am still unsettled over climbing the mountains."

"With your condition, I'm sure you will suffer in the mountains the most," Libbie said. "Yet again, it will just be hard as there is more than one, the Grey Mountains."

I sighed deeply. Sulleth planned to use Vex. I was sure of it. Yet I was also sure that Vex was planning to use Sulleth. Which one that would be successful existed as a mystery to me. Suddenly, I realised Libbie was just watching me, waiting for some sort of reply.

"Errm, yeah, I agree."

"Okay." Libbie then walked away.

Still walking next to my pals, I considered what Sulleth's plan for me was. He consistently mentioned having plans for me, in which I had no clue what they were, yet they must be of some importance to hasten the occurrence of a death prophecy. Sure enough, fear was seeping through my veins of what they would do to my friends if they caught us.

No, Ace, don't think of such things! I thought to myself. Even though I knew that no animals or forces of the empire could see us, I still got a sense of someone watching me.

"Ace," Becky said. "It seems we will have to scrap your plan."

"Why?" I questioned.

"Well, quite obvious reasons," Becky continued. "We have no more food."

"Great," I mumbled quietly. "I shall ask Chorus where the nearest settlement is."

I then asked Chorus within my head, in which I shall not repeat said conversation as you probably got the jist. "The nearest settlement is a few more miles north, yet Chorus warns us of some unexpected surprises."

"Can you ask it?" Austin asked.

"No, Chorus always is saying that we must discover things for ourselves, whatever that means."

"Okay, let's get going then. Full steam ahead!" Becky said. We pushed through the snow, which I could tell was beginning to thicken and become more blizzard-like, if that's a term. After a few miles worth of walking, we arrived at the town, and Chorus was right, there were some unexpected surprises. It seemed that it was a border town, as half of the settlement was frozen in the ice wall.

"Wasn't what I was expecting…" Jim said. As we entered the settlement, we noticed that the town was abandoned. No creatures of any kind were in sight, and many parts of the town had collapsed letting the snow in. Still, the most breath stealing part was still the fact that half of the town had been frozen within the ice wall. Some of the buildings had burnt down also. Even the wind seemed quieter here. All I heard was the deep breathing of my friends.

"Guys, draw your weapons, I feel like something edgy is gonna happen."

I then heard the unsheathing of swords, which was my friends drawing their harpes. I also summoned Chorus' blade form. We strolled through the town, trying to look for a store. When I spied one, I said, "Here, follow," which my friends did indeed do. We entered. It was much like a regular house, except with shelves, lots and lots of shelves.

These shelves though were mouldy and what I thought would be out of date foods, however, some unnatural things were upon these shelves. Upon the shelves, there were also nasty blood stains, severed heads, an open coffin with knives impaled on the inside. There were dead bodies scattered everywhere.

They looked like regular dead, non-warrior Exelon empire zombies, which varied in appearance, some were full skeletons while some were half eaten corpses, et cetera.

Then a loud bang echoed through the store.

Chapter 15

We turned quickly towards the noise. It seemed not to be within the first floor of the building.

"Guys, I think it's upstairs," I told the others. Treading carefully and quietly through the desolate store, we listened out for another clatter, or even footsteps.

"Let's go up the stairs," Becky said after we spied a staircase. Again, near silently, we walked through the store towards the stairs. We began the ascent towards the second floor.

Once we reached the next storey, I looked around. The second floor was more crowded with fallen cupboards and artefacts. Less bodies were on the floor, yet more blood stains existed.

"Okay, Becky, you come with me. Jim, Libbie, Austin, you guys go as a three," I whispered to them. Once we split up, we ventured into the labyrinth-like room. No more noises could be heard during the exploration but an eerie amount of blood was stained into the floor, even though the bodies where the blood originated from could not be seen.

"Maybe it was another Rimoor animal?" Becky said.

"Doubtfully," I replied. "Chorus said barely any animals were around the place when we set off from last night's camp."

"Then who could it be, or what?"

"Maybe the assassins…"

"It couldn't be, why would the assassins kill so many people and topple over the things in the room. It's not logical, locking themselves within the room," she said.

"That makes sense," I said.

Another noise echoed within the floor, but this time the noise seemed closer. I edged closer and peeked around the corner. And I saw a ghastly thing.

Becky peeked around the corner. I held her mouth shut to hold in her scream, the same as I was doing to myself. It had marble white skin with no specific texture. It was also roughly six inches smaller than me, which suited the creature because of how thin it was. It was so thin that you could have seen every single bone in its spine. Where the creature sat was in the centre of a chamber, which connected into another room.

"Ssssstop clattering around, Darf."

A painful remembrance of the voice resonated in me. "S-s-s-sorry, mistress," moaned the thin creature which I think was called Darf. Serpias then slithered around the corner and out of the connecting room. She was down so that her waist almost touched the floor, as to fit inside the room.

"Sssso, do you know if they are here?" Serpias asked Darf.

"Y-y-yes, M'lady."

"Sssso, are they?" Serpias asked, beginning to gain an impatient tone in her voice.

"They are h-here, M'lady. I-I-I think they are within this very building."

"Very good, Darf."

"S-s-so I have laid out the room to be like a maze. I can tell that since I made the noise, they w-will be coming up h-h-here," Darf continued. "I th-th-think they w-w-w-will be lost by n-now."

"That isssss very good, Darf. Thossse wretched children musssst pay for desssstroying my home."

"Teenagers," I mumbled in my breath. I thought about how she must think reality works. She tries to eat us, we destroy her home. Fair's fair. Then a dreaded thing happened. I heard a cough from my friends in the other explorer group. Serpias turned with such motion that it would have given a regular human a head rush. She automatically slithered away into the maze, after the source of the cough.

"S-S-S-Serpias, M'lady, what about the others?" Darf said. But by the time he finished the sentence, Serpias had already slithered too far into the maze, with her tail still leaving the room where she came from. Darf suddenly stood up and began to waddle the way me and Becky were hiding. For a waddle though, Darf was extremely fast.

"Run!" I whispered to Becky.

Myself in tow, I followed Becky further into the toppled maze-room.

"I H-H-HEAR YOU!" Darf shouted. I turned around to look behind me and already saw Darf waddling around the corner following me and Becky. "NOW I S-SEE YOU!" Darf cried again, picking up more speed. I turned in front of me and saw Becky turn a corner suddenly. With the momentum I was going at, I fell over as I made the turn.

Getting up with such speed, I sped towards Becky. Following her through the maze, I could hear Darf breathing deeply. I turned around again and saw Darf frog leaping after me. I then heard shouts and screams from further away in the maze, probably my friends seeing Serpias chasing after them. I hoped with all my heart that they turned tails and ran away from Serpias.

"Why!" I shouted with obvious sadness. I followed Becky again, catching up enough to be right next to her. I could tell that Darf was catching up because I could hear his breathing louder than ever. We came across a sideways cupboard, which me and Becky climbed over. Once we did so, we ran as fast as possible. I turned around to see Darf further back, having just climbed down from the cupboard.

We had given ourselves a huge distance from Darf. We then came across a T-section in the maze, where we saw the others run across, then saw Serpias only a metre behind following them.

"We gotta backtrack!" I told Becky.

We ran back and into another side lane. I could hear Darf closing in behind us.

"Go!" I shouted to Becky. As she zoomed off, Darf landed and grabbed my back. I turned rapidly trying to shake Darf off. He crawled over my head and somehow pulled me to the ground. He climbed over me and opened his mouth. His human-like teeth retracted and out produced another layer of teeth, six inch teeth sharpened to the likes of a dagger.

Opening his mouth wider, he moved his head sideways about to bite my neck. I quickly headbutted Darf in his nose. He fell backwards from me, weeping on the floor. I got up and ran, ran as quickly as possible. I turned many times and turned a corner.

Suddenly, I heard all of the other guys scream in unison. I looked behind me to see my friends closing in on my back. Once they reached my side, we ran towards a brick wall.

"Ace! What are you doing?" Austin screamed.

"Trust me!" I said.

I put Chorus in front of me and willed for, well, I don't know what really, but I willed for *something* to happen. Then me and my companions jumped right through the brick wall, the bricks flying out of its location. We landed rolling. Hurriedly, I got up and pulled my friends to their feet.

"Good job," mumbled Jim.

"Praise me later," I replied. I looked towards the wall to see Darf and Serpias coming through it.

"Yeah, I'll praise you later," Jim said, taking off north. Me, Becky, Libbie, and Austin in close tow. We left the half frozen town and continued running. I fell behind on purpose and thought *energy.* A beam of golden energy emitted from the tip of the blade which hit Serpias and Darf. Looking forward again, I pulsed myself towards the others.

"Guys, get in," I said, while using Chorus to magically conjure a small underground den, like a hole. The others climbed in, me being the last. I then used Chorus to cover the entrance to the hole with a fresh patch of grass, also ordering Chorus to fill the grass patch with snow, so as to not look suspicious.

"Stay quiet," I whispered to the others. The hole was a tight fit, having conjured it in a hurry. In silence we listened intently for the sound of Serpias and Darf. Suddenly, the sound of something heavy dragging itself across the floor appeared, also with the sound of little feet running. The sound stopped, seemingly right above where we were.

I heard muffled voices, obviously the voice of Serpias and the mumbling voice of Darf. As quickly as the monsters came, they left, the direction which they were heading in being north.

"You think they're gone?" Austin whispered.

"Yeah," I replied near silently.

I used Chorus' magic to blast away the magical patch of earth that covered the entrance to the hole. I poked my head out, looking in all directions. I climbed out and gave the all clear to the others. I turned Chorus into a bracelet.

"Oh god, that was close," Libbie said.

"Hmm," I replied thinking deeply about the occurrence.

"Let's go," I said.

We continued north, following the ice wall. "Ace, you are contemplating the town," Chorus said. I walked in front of the others to communicate with Chorus more privately.

"Yeah, I am. What even was that place?" I asked.

Chorus replied saying, "It was a border town for the kingdoms of Rimoor and Ambrian."

"What happened to it?" I continued asking.

"Well, half the town is Rimoor owned while the other half was Ambrians, so when the Exelon empire took over, and used the Blizzard stone to isolate the kingdom from the outer world, magic refused to curve out the way of a single settlement. The ice wall grew out of the ground in the middle of the settlement, causing the Ambrian half of the town to be frozen within the new borders of Rimoor."

"But why was it burnt, it seemed like someone had committed arson within the town and began a town sized fire?"

"Ahh well," Chorus said sadly. "When the town was frozen, it rebelled against the empire, which led to the Exelon empire coming forth and destroying the Rimoor half of the town."

"That's horrible," I said.

"I know."

"So what was Darf?" I questioned further.

"Ahh, you know how you humans shorten names to make it easier to talk with them," Chorus said.

"Yes."

"Well, Darf is short for Darfinian."

"Darf was *human*," I said shocked.

"Yes, Darf, as far as I can tell, was the town's mayor, and when the empire took over, it used ancient black sorcery to turn him into what you saw him as. Of course, he was driven insane by the magic."

"That's so evil!" I said.

"I know, that is the cruelty of Vex and his army," Chorus replied.

"Is there any way to free Darf of his curse?"

"Sadly enough, there is not. Black sorcery is not like a regular curse, it is much older, far more terrible. The curse that rested upon Darf is the Couliactus infection, a magical disease that drives the host insane, making them into crazed monsters."

"But there is always a cure, somewhere…" I said.

"In your realm perhaps, yet Rimoor is a far more vicious place where only the strongest survive." Unsettling silence settled upon myself and Chorus.

"Can you at least tell me how Serpias got in front of us?" I asked.

"That I can," Chorus said. "Serpias is that of an old civilisation of dune dwellers, native to the kingdom of Durmin, where only deserts exist. When the Knights of Eternalis Brotherhood moved from Evenar to Durmin, beginning their rise to form the first ever religious empire, Serpias' species was wiped almost to extinction. It appeared that Serpias was the last of her species and in a last desperate attempt, fled from Durmin to Rimoor, where she dwells still."

"The last bit I figured, with her still being in the kingdom, as well, we just saw her," I said. "But that doesn't answer my question."

"Very magical creatures, the citizens of Durmin, they may be uncivilised but very magically connected and far more bodily superior. They can last longer building their monuments and cities, they can spend long time running, or in Serpias' case, slithering. You can see where I am heading."

"Yes," I replied.

"In truth you overestimate Serpias."

I replied saying, "Overestimate?"

"Indeed, the Knights of Eternalis Brotherhood succeeded in creating the very first holy empire, having conquered Durmin and Evenar. They follow far more…magical concepts, black sorcery mainly. This makes their empire a few more steps larger than the Exelon empire, meaning the forces of the Exelon empire could beat Serpias with ease."

"And with us having beat forces of the Exelon empire, we could beat Serpias?" I asked.

"Well, Serpias is very strong and unforgiving, but she is not very smart."

"Then how did her species make cities as you just said?"

Chorus suddenly buzzed in my hand, almost as if it was raising an eyebrow. "You did hear what I said right?" Chorus said.

I realised my stupidity. "Yeah, I get it now. Durmin is full of different species including Serpias' species and that of others."

"Humans live in Durmin, yet they are like a different breed of human. They are intelligent but not as much as humans from Rimoor, but they are stronger than humans from Rimoor."

"Okay," I said. "So you're saying we can use Serpias' unintelligence to kill her?" I asked.

"Precisely," Chorus said.

I breathed in and out deeply. I looked behind me to see my friends talking. Then I slowed down to let the others catch up to me. "What were you talking about?" Jim asked.

"Just stuff," I said.

"Uhhm, okay," he replied.

I got the feeling that he knew that I didn't want him to press further. I felt like telling the others what I just heard would simply put their minds out of their comfort zone. I looked forward again and walked further north with the ice wall to our left.

After a while of walking, we came across a small forest, which I could tell was small because through the trees, I could see the end of it. However, I began to have no faith in forests since the forest of imagination. A shiver went down my spine as I thought of it.

It isn't that far, Ace, you can do it! said the positive little voice inside my head. The darker, negative voice inside my head was like, *You never know what might be in there, Ace, could be a small forest of imagination.* I mentally swatted aside the little devil and went with the positive angel in my head (come on, that comparison is hilarious!).

"Guys, we can get through the forest, we can see the end of it, just nobody wander off," I told them.

"Okay, just don't wander off by yourself then," Libbie countered.

"I won't," I replied.

Off we strode into the woods. A quarter of the way there. Halfway there. A quarter left to walk. We reached the end of the small forest. I let out a sigh.

"You all right?" I asked.

"Yeah," said the others. I smiled and then I fell face first into the snow.

I opened my eyes to see Vex. He was on top of a fortress outside the Capital Land (As there were no buildings in sight, of course except for the fortress). He watched as roughly fifty golem warriors marched out a huge arch that led into the fortress, with another two hundred zombie warriors escorting them. "Production is going well then," said Lord Vex in his usual drawling voice.

"Very," said a man in emerald, fur lined robes.

"I hope that you have prepared my carriage back into the Capital Land," replied Vex.

"Yes, Emperor. However, the thought of having a long journey carriage for only a five mile trip sounds quite unnecessary," said the robed man.

"Do not question me," Vex replied.

The robed man then replied saying, "I hope I haven't annoyed you, sire, as we have known each other for many years."

"Our friendship has benefited you, Sariqua, me making you governor of Redstone fortress."

"I am aware and grateful, sire."

"That is good. Now I shall take my leave and board my carriage," Vex finalised.

"I really do enjoy you visiting Redstone fortress, it is an honour and enjoyment."

"You shall be departing north-west tomorrow at sunrise," Vex said.

"Why?" Sariqua said with a surprised tone.

"I am in need of a centre island governor to head to the Goblin's sea. As you are only seventy miles away from the coast, I have chosen you," Vex said.

"I say with all gratitude that I must decline the offer, it seems unfit to me," the other replied. Vex then began to walk to the doorway which led to the inside of the fortress. He clicked his tongue and suddenly, his two hyenas bounded out of the doorway and ate Sariqua.

As Vex entered the dry fortress, he told a door butler, "Have Governor Arich notified that he is now the governor of Redstone fortress and that he will be departing to make a peace treaty with the goblin pirates in the sea. Oh, and clean up the mess outside." Vex then continued to walk, his hyenas suddenly stopping their feast and following their master.

114

The vision suddenly dissolved into mist and began to swirl. The mist reformed into a different scene in a different location. Serpias was curled up inside a medium sized cave with Darf sitting next to a blazing fire. Anyone there could easily hear the howl of the wind and see the blast of the blizzard.

"Serpias, why don't we head back to the town and wait there until the storm is over?" Darf said, almost unaware of the unending blizzard at the mouth of the cave. Serpias' eyes suddenly flickered open and became fixed on Darf.

"You *are* aware of the magical curse that has bestowed itself upon this land?" Serpias asked with a questioning tone.

Darf's eyes suddenly rolled up into his head and back down. "Yes, my lady," he replied sadly.

Serpias then hissed and spoke, "You deeply confussse me, Darf. I have seen unsssspeakable things in my lifetime and vassstly confusing thingsss, yet you are sssomething that even attacks the very sssanity of my mind, or what'ssss left of it anywayssss."

"I confuse myself, m'lady."

"Well, that issss unsssetling even for me," Serpias mumbled. "Well, at leassst the humans that dessstroyed my mini-desert are nearing Chalin fortresssss, we can continue our assssault there."

"The fortress protecting the near northern barrier?" Darf asked.

"Yesss, of courssse, Darf. Didn't you pick up on anything I dissscovered earlier?"

"Yes, my lady," Darf replied, hanging his head down in sorrow.

"Sssoon, ever ssso sssoon." Serpias laughed. Darf began to laugh, until Serpias told him, "Quiet!"

"Sorry," Darf replied. (I was afraid at the time but nowadays when I remember what I saw, it makes me laugh with the movie like quality.) The scene dissolved into mist like the previous vision and I suddenly snapped awake. I looked up to see that it was night.

Then I realised that I was in the same place as I had been when I fainted. I looked forward to the other four to see them fast asleep.

"No no no." I stumbled as I crawled over to Becky's side. I checked her pulse (as I had learnt to do in P.E.) and saw that she was still alive. Still in fear, I summoned Chorus and asked it something.

"Okay, are all the forests in this kingdom demonic?"

"No, Ace, it's just a coincidence that you and your friends have run right into two really bad ones," Chorus replied.

"Okay, so what is the evil quality in this one?" I asked.

Chorus hummed for a moment before answering. "That is the woods of the drunk."

"Why do I have a feeling that those woods aren't as merry as they sound?"

"Well, the woods of the drunk was a regular forest that became cursed when the first ever drunk person died within it."

"Okay so!" I asked urgently.

"Well, the curse causes anyone who passes through it to go into a very very deep sleep."

"How deep?" I asked.

"So deep that you could live an entire life inside it," Chorus replied. "It is only as long as a regular dream though,

116

but when most people wake up, they are driven insane by the fact that the life they just lived is that of a lie."

"So what can I do?" I again asked.

"Burn down the forest."

"But won't that, like, destroy loads of life here."

"No, it will just burn away the curse, the forest shall be lifted of its curse while it stays intact." I stood up without hesitation and used Chorus to fire a fireball at the trees. I looked down to see Becky's eyes flick open and Vex's eyes existing inside her sockets. Then I actually woke up...

I sat up so quickly, I got a head rush.

"Arrgh!" I shouted as I laid back down. I was dripping in frozen sweat. I didn't even know that that was possible! Then Chorus said in my head, "Ace! Good, you are awake."

"What happened?" I mumbled.

"Once you exited the forest, you fainted."

"I figured that."

"You seemed to go into a vision, two I believe. Then you had a normal, human dream."

"So the forest isn't cursed?" I asked.

"Oh, no, it isn't," replied Chorus.

"Thank the god of this universe!" I said.

"By that, I do not think that you are supposing Rince in a more literal way, I suppose you are using that as a figurative way."

"Still getting used to human ways of speaking?"

"Yes."

"Okay." I got up and used Chorus, even in its bracelet form, to get rid of the icy sweat. Once I was cleaned up, I left my room and exited the tent.

"Hi! Come sit down," Jim said to me. The campfire was still in full blaze and it was already day.

"You gonna tell us about your dreams then?" Libbie asked.

"Oh, yeah," I said. I then went on to tell them about the two visions (not the dream as I only viewed it as a nightmare).

"Okay, so the first vision seems of less importance at the moment in time, but the second vision seems to be more significant," Austin said.

"Yes, I agree. An entire fortress guarding the ice wall in the north, that is gonna be hard to get through," Becky said. They then went on to tell me that once I fainted, they set up the camp and set me down inside the tent.

"Thanks," I told them, grateful for the fact that they did such things.

"It's completely alright," Libbie said.

"So an entire fortress. How large?" Jim asked.

"I'm not sure, all I know is that there is one. I didn't see the actual fortress," I replied.

"So we are taking the word of Serpias and Darf?" Jim asked.

"I guess so, but we must take all possible precautions about this," I said.

"True," Becky said.

"So, now what?" Austin wondered aloud.

"We continue what we have already been doing, heading north and fighting our way out of any major issue," I replied.

"You and Chorus have been talking more than usual. Is there something that you want to tell us?" Libbie furthered.

Myself, being now stuck in a very, very sticky situation had no other choice but to do something I thought I would never have to do on the quest. I lied to them. "No, it is just mainly how much further we have to go."

"Good," Becky whispered.

"Let's get going then," I told the others.

We then continued to pack up the tent and head north. "ACE!" Chorus shouted angrily in my mind.

I then talked to it inside my head, "What?"

"You LIED!"

"Yeah, I know."

"The only way to get through this quest without failure is no lies. By lying, you are nearing the path that Sulleth went down."

I gulped nervously. "I just don't want the others to be screwed up by the fact of everything you have told me."

"This is a very stressful time for you, Ace, but stop LYING!"

"Sorry, I won't do it again."

"That's right, you won't!" It was the first time Chorus had seemed mad, and if I am to be honest, it was so scary.

"No more lies," I mumbled aloud.

"What?" asked Austin.

"Oh, nothing," I replied hurriedly.

"All right, I will let this one sit but make sure you tell no more lies," Chorus said.

"Okay," I replied within my mind.

"Are you talking with Chorus again?" Libbie asked.

"Yes, I was having a conversation with it about honesty." I mentally hoped Libbie would not push further.

"All right," Libbie said. Then out of the blinding snow came the image of a town, and it had the Exelon empire flag hanging on the walls.

Chapter 16

"Get down!" I told the others. We all fell down to our stomachs. The town was surrounded by high, pure black walls with Exelon empire banners hanging from them. Also, on the walls, there were huge iron doors. Oh, by the way, the empires' symbol is much like the Buddhist dharma wheel symbol but it is pure black with a crimson background.

"Is this the fortress?" Jim whispered, crawling to my left.

"I don't think so, I think it is just a very protected town," I whispered back. Zombie warriors patrolled the walls.

"So now what? Should we go around?" Becky asked, crawling to my right.

"No," I replied. "I don't think our appearances are known by the empire, we are simply like passers-by to them."

"So you want to enter the enemy ruled town?" Jim asked. Suddenly, the huge iron doors opened. Out came a blonde, curly haired man with a clean shaven face and electric blue eyes. He was wearing chainmail with a sort of buttonless black trench coat.

Hanging down his front was an Exelon empire banner, much like a reversed cape. Hanging at his side was an iron war-hammer which had the appearance of a staff with a fist gripping a large circular dumbbell. Behind him were ten bodyguards in shadowy armour and wielding fyeahswords in a shotel style. He walked directly towards us. "Get up, children!" He barked in a commanding tone. Me and the other four began to stand up. "Quicker!"

Once we were standing up straight, Austin asked, "So, we are people from this town, we just heard a really huge…yowl, so we went to check it out." I thanked the goddess Rince that Austin came up with that story, silently of course.

"Well, take this as an honour, I am Count Charles. I keep control of the town." He waved his left hand over his shoulder. The bodyguards suddenly sheathed their blades. "You may also know me from your tutors, I am the one that helped normalise Exelon rule out here in the outer kingdom. I actually am the one that destroyed that town down south."

My eyes suddenly flicked open so wide that you could probably think my pupils were black holes. "You are the one that destroyed the town down south, the one that bordered Rimoor and Ambrian?" I asked.

"Yes. How you know that the town further south is a border town is quite concerning." He must have mentally flicked aside the factor as he did not push further with any questions. "Come, we shall dine before I send you back to your parents," Count Charles concluded. He turned rapidly and walked back to the gates, the bodyguards marching at his sides.

"Come on," I told the others. They were probably in equal shock as to how easy it was to infiltrate the town. Me and my friends then followed the Count. Once we entered the town, the doors closed much too fast for their size. Once my attention was taken away from the gates, my mind was blown.

There were statues, house sized castles, weapon stores, a military camp, a park and even a sort of jewellery shop.

We pressed on through the town until we came across some iron gates. They opened as me, my friends, the bodyguards and the Count approached. Once we entered, like the doors, the gates closed. There was a freaky fountain which had frozen, so the fauns that spewed forth the water from their flutes were actually spewing out long, concentrated jets of ice that followed in a singular beam until it reached the frozen water at the base of the fountain.

We went around the fountain and entered a house. As I said, there were house sized castles, the building in which we entered was a castle sized house. Of course a smaller castle, as a full on castle sized house would have been much larger. The Count then pushed the fir tree doors open himself, letting the blizzard in. Once we entered, he closed the doors and clicked his fingers.

Suddenly, what I thought would have been an abandoned mansion (as the building had no furniture or decoration or any warmth) turned into a very homey place. The house seemed to emit warmth and out of the walls and floors came squishy furniture and artwork.

"Wow," Libbie said.

"Never seen magic before?" The Count asked.

"Oh, I have, just not something like, like *this*!" Libbie replied.

"Come," said Count Charles. Us and the bodyguards followed Charles further into the house. We then came across a hallway, which seemed unnatural to the rest of the house. Unlike the homey, cosy feel of the house, the hallway was literally a dungeon. Built into the walls were holding cells, and at the end of the hallway was a staircase.

My mind was racing, saying *HE'S GONNA TRAP YOU INTO A CELL! RUN!* Yet, I did not. We then walked down the hallway, seeing many people in a range of tortures. I saw one person who was so thin, she seemed to have no muscle or flesh or organs. Another one was a really fat human with a conveyor belt with food piled onto it coming from the back wall of the cell and into his back.

He was crying, "Let me go! Do you know who I am! I am Donnie Flickson!"

"Don't mind him, he was an old noble who I had punished," the Count said. Just when I thought the guy could have been a nice person. We then climbed the staircase and into a dining hall.

"Sit," said Count Charles. Me and my friends sat down and looked as the Count sat at the head of the table. The bodyguards then proceeded to exit the room via a side door. Food was already set upon the table. "Eat," said Charles. He then proceeded to tell us a story, while me and the others, including the Count piled food onto our plates.

After a while, something the Count said really spiked my attention. "Well, my rank is Count, meaning I am higher rank than peasants and non-Exelon nobles, but I am not higher than governor. I am much harder working than Governor Frederick but I am still not a higher rank. I swear it is all to do with Frederick, the Vicious, and Emperor Vex having a strong friendship."

"That's *another* thing I don't understand, why does Governor Frederick have the nickname 'Frederick, the Vicious'. If he has a nickname, surely should I!"

"Yeah totally, I am all onboard with you deserving to have the title governor and a nickname," I said. I am not siding with the empire, all I was doing was playing the part of being a brainwashed peasant within the ranks of the Exelon empire.

"And Frederick, the Vicious, is the governor for Chalin fortress," said the Count, completely dismissing what I said. Then it hit me. Chalin fortress, that was the name of the fortress that guarded the northern ice walls. Me and my fellows were going to have to face someone nicknamed the Vicious.

"Nevermind the fact that Chalin fortress is the second most feared fortress out there, the first being the Redstone fortress. Redstone fortress literally has a golem warrior farm under it. Well, actually, the Capital Land nowadays is a city wide fortress, so that makes Redstone fortress the second most feared one and Chalin, the third." He chuckled at the thought. "Well, tell us about your life?"

I looked towards Austin, the story king of the day. "Well, surprisingly enough, we all come from one family," Austin said.

"Really? It seems very unlikely because of your appearance difference."

"Yeah, like it's random, but life is life," replied Austin. He was slowly losing his grip on the story.

"Haven't I seen you before?" Count Charles said.

"No, not that I'm aware of," I said.

"Hmmm." I could almost see the Count's mind working. "I shall let you leave after the meal. I see you of no main interest." He grimaced as he said it. He turned from a more or less merry person to being a bored person. Once we finished our meal, he stood up.

"Well, goodbye," Becky said.

The Count then clicked his fingers and out of the side doors came the bodyguards, drawing their shotel fyeahswords. "I don't think so." He then grinned so broadly he seemed like a demon. "You are the Exelon rebels." He then pointed to me. "You are the champion of Rince, wielder of the gift of Rince."

Count Charles then pointed to each of my other four friends individually. "And these are your accomplices." He laughed. "I shall have you imprisoned, then I shall have Lord Vex brought here. I shall go down in Exelon history."

I attempted to summon Chorus, yet my bracelet did not transform. The guards then reached us and grappled our arms and pushed us down the stairs. They then opened the cell doors and pushed us in.

"Such glory," Libbie said.

"Yeah, definitely," I said sarcastically.

"So now what? We just wait here. Ace, use Chorus to break us out," Becky said.

I then attempted to summon Chorus, yet again it did not work. "It ain't working," I said.

Chorus then said within my mind, "Ace, you are in a magical box."

"A magical box?" I replied out loud.

"What?" Jim said.

"Oh, nothing."

"Yes, a magical box. It retains all magical bonds and connections, meaning even god-like powers which we hold cannot work," Chorus then said still in my head.

I then replied silently, "How though? Does this mean Rince would be retained?"

"No, she is a goddess. It won't work with us because my magic is filtered down, so mortals such as yourself can wield me."

I then said out loud to my friends, "Did they take your swords?"

All of my friends then reached into their winter jackets and pulled out their harpes. "No," Becky said. The ambient noise of the other prisoners being tortured was disturbing my thinking.

"Try poking the swords through the gaps in the bars." Austin then stood up and attempted to poke his sword in between the bars. The blade didn't even partially go through the gap, like an invisible barrier was in between each bar. Austin then sheathed his harpe while saying, "Nah, this isn't working." He then slumped back onto the floor.

I then looked behind me at the stone wall at the back of the cell. Studying it carefully, I saw no crack or dent. Chorus then said aloud, "Don't you see it?"

"How do *you* see it, Chorus, you have no eyes," I said to my bracelet. "I can't see anything," I continued.

"Bah, look to the bottom right hand corner of the cell," Chorus then said. I looked and saw a small gap leading somewhere. I then crawled down to my chest and looked through it. It led into another room, that room having an open window. I then looked around to every single cell, each had one.

"Guys, don't worry, I'm going to try something," I told the four. I then poked my index finger through the hole into the other room. I felt a tingle run through the finger nail that was poking through. "It's the world's smallest air vent," I whispered to myself. "Chorus, is my fingernail free from the magical box?"

"It seems so, yes," replied Chorus.

"Guys, I'm gonna come back for you," I said.

I then willed Chorus to turn my body into a type of slime. It happened. It was weird, being an unsolid form. I felt free yet constrained in a very tight box. I then attempted to move myself. I slithered along the ground and moulded into a very tight shape. I slithered through the hole, feeling even more restricted because of the tightness of the hole.

Once my entire goo form had made it through the gap, I slumped with a very wet noise onto the ground. I then continued to slither across the room and to the open window, which I shaped myself through. Once I made it to the outer courtyard of the mansion, I reformed into my original body.

"Even I have never done that before," Chorus said.

"Yeah…" I really didn't know how to finish that sentence. I then summoned Chorus into its sword form while crouching and walking along the side of the mansion. The snow was battering my face, putting me off from my decision making. Once I had made it to the front door of the mansion, I pushed the door open, walked in and closed it.

I stood up and walked quietly along the corridor. From plain memory, I walked through the house until I made it into the prison cell hallway. "Ace!" Libbie shouted. I walked over to my friends and magically unlocked their cells, from the outside of course, where the magical box didn't affect me. They then unsheathed their harpes and followed me to the front door.

I tried to push the thought of the prisoners out of my mind. If I had attempted to save them, one of the house guards would have noticed. Our primary mission was the quest. Once we had walked to the outside of the house, I noticed a small door that was to the left of the mansion, built into the wall. I walked towards it, when from the front door came the bodyguards, fully armed with their swords.

"Are you kidding me…" I mumbled under my breath. The guards didn't run, they just marched after us. I prepared Chorus, my friends drawing their harpes. We ran towards them, blades raised, the guards then carried on to bring their blades down at such timing, they almost cut off our heads. Luckily, we all ducked under the strike.

I hurriedly stabbed one of the ten guards just at the bottom of their lungs. They then toppled. The other ten guards then swept their hands in unison and the compound became shrouded in a darkness so thick, one could have mistaken it for the blackest of nights. I looked around rapidly, only to return my eyesight to where the guards were. They had seemingly disappeared in the shadows.

I looked around, my friends frantically doing the same thing. Suddenly, all of the guards rose from the solid rock ground, as if they were a ghost rising from the floor. It was so quick, I could hardly process it. They rose and slashed their blades in a wide arc like motion. They then walked forwards. I attempted to stab one of them, but just before my sword touched the guards armour, the being sunk into the ground.

I turned around, as I had anticipated where they would rise next. Suddenly, like before, the guards rose from the ground at such speeds, I could hardly read their movements. I stabbed just as its chest had reached sword level, however, the bodyguards did a sneaky counter movement where they sank back into the dark ground. I stumbled forward, Chorus falling to my side.

Then the guard I was fighting rose from the ground and cut my left arm. I stumbled to the right, looking at my cut arm. It was a deep wound and it was weeping a green puss. The blades must have been poisoned. I turned tails and ran towards the door. "Ace, where are you going!" One of my friends called whose identity was hidden from the headache that followed the blade gash.

"Run!" I shouted! My voice, even though I was trying to shout, seemed near silent. As I neared the door, from the side of my vision I could see one of the guards walking out of the compound wall. Once I reached the door, I opened it and walked through a very tight tunnel. I looked up.

The colour of the compound's sky then shifted from black (made black I believe by making a spell) to a greyish white, like the Rimoor day (as I had known it). I looked behind me to see my friends close in tow to me.

Once we made it out of the tunnel, and out of the Exelon ruled town, I blanked out.

Chapter 17

I woke up at a river bank, throwing up with such ferocity, I was afraid I may die of being too thin. Once I finished, I looked behind me and around me to see my friends settled around at the camp. We were in a small clearing within a forest.

"Where am I?" I whispered to Chorus.

"Well, once you blanked out, I controlled your body and led you into this forest, to this river, so you could upchuck all of the poison that had reached your stomach," Chorus said in a patient tone.

"I really don't wanna know how those guards were able to ghostify through the floor," I mumbled.

"Ahh, well, the guards seemed not from this kingdom," said my sword, ignoring what I had said.

"Where were they from?" I asked, in a quiet tone.

"They were knights from Evenar."

"How did they get here?" I pushed.

"It seems that they snuck in here once the Knights of Eternalis Brotherhood conquered Durmin. I guess that they were analysing Rimoor for a possible conquest. They could faze through the shadows, its black sorcery, magic that only works in dark environments."

"Yeah..." I mumbled, only half aware of what Chorus was saying.

"My most understandable and feasible idea about this is that they cast a magical shadow dome over the manor and used their dark magic transportation to travel like they did."

"Ehhh." I gripped Chorus' hilt, as the blade was lying to my right. Once I had stood up, instinct told me to do something. I jabbed sideways. I didn't look, I didn't even feel, I just sensed that I should. I heard a grunt and the sound of something heavy falling onto the floor.

Time to que the epic music. I turned to my right to see Chorus impaled in Count Charles' heart. On the floor next to him was his war-hammer.

"H-how," he mumbled before he fell back, falling away from Chorus. I mentally ordered Chorus to be clean, which it did. Austin, Becky, Libbie and Jim ran up beside me.

"We heard the grunt," Libbie said.

I looked around and I could not see the dead Count's bodyguards. I walked towards the dead body and picked up the hammer.

"Libbie, here," I said while raising the hammer.

"What?" She said, startled.

"The hammer, I think it will suit you, at least give it a try," I replied. Libbie then walked forward and took the hammer from me. She then went on to hang the war-hammer on her belt.

"You're right, the weapon does suit her," Jim said in awe. "Stay on guard," I said. "If Charles was able to find us, his guards could." I walked towards the campfire. I sat down on a log and thought.

I was wondering how we would get past Chalin fortress, all the while being now known appearance wise. I closed my eyes for a second, only to open them in a different scene. Vex was sat upon his throne, with the remaining assassins in front of him.

"Tut tut," Vex mumbled disapprovingly.

"My lord, we swear upon our parents' lives that they bested us," said one of the assassins. Vex clicked his fingers. One of the six guards to the side of him walked forwards and lowered their spear to one of the assassin's gut. A blast of purple fire emitted from the spear tip, which disintegrated the assassin that spoke, even the weapons were reduced to atoms.

"Such disappointment. I thought that you were my best warriors," Vex said.

"We still are, my lord. The earthlings that wield the gift of Rince, they are simply overpowering us."

"CHILDREN! THEY ARE JUST CHILDREN!" Vex shouted. He did this while banging his left hand upon his throne's left armrest. "YOU CAN TAKE DOWN MANY OF MY GOLEM WARRIORS ALONE, YET YOU STILL CANNOT BEAT FIVE PUNY, ADOLESCENT CHILDREN!" Vex continued.

Two more of Vex's guards stepped forwards, lowering their spears like the first, and obliterated the rest of the assassins until only two remained.

"My lord, we shall succeed in our next attempt at assassination," said one of the remaining two assassins.

Vex replied, "Of course you will, unless you wish to end up like your ex-colleagues."

"Yes," said the other.

"Vladimir Flamanofff, Semala Tricht. Do not fail me," Vex finalised. I then opened my eyes again. My friends were sitting on the logs, laughing, talking.

"Hey, guys, listen up." I then told them what I had seen.

"That is crazy, like you seemed regular, just sat there, blinking. You just seemed...thinky?" Austin replied, saying the last word as a question.

"Austin, if you want to know, thinky isn't a word," I said. If I'm to be honest, I don't actually know if thinky is a word or not.

"Okay thanks," Austin said.

"Quite alright," I said, still contemplating if thinky is a word.

"So there are only two assassins left, Serpias and Darf. And of course the Exelon empire," Becky said.

"Don't think too much about the final one, if we focus on Serpias, Darf and the assassins, we might not go insane," I replied.

"Ehh, shouldn't we have already gone insane?" Jim asked.

"I really don't know now," I mumbled.

"*Cal!*" Sulleth suddenly said within my mind. A new sense of depression settled over me. The thought of Cal still being slowly murdered inside one of those golem warriors echoed inside me.

Later, I realised how hungry all of us were, and since we were all out of food, I had to take matters into my own hands.

"Don't do it," warned Austin.

"You wanna go hungry? Ehh," I replied.

"You got him there," laughed Libbie.

"Okay, if I don't come back up in another ten minutes, well, don't think too much of it, I might be completing the quest alone," I joked.

The others gave me a glare saying, *Don't joke about such things!* I gulped. I then looked at the river that was somehow not frozen.

"Alright Ace, be careful, this is a sort of volcano fuelled river. For once we have to be glad that it is cold, otherwise when you plunge into it, you would boil," Chorus said within my mind. I gulped again. Then I jumped into the river. It was far deeper than I would have anticipated. I swam further down, aware that it was more likely to find fish nearer the bottom, which had to be warmer.

As I sank deeper, it seemed to get lighter. It made no sense, surely the deeper I went, the darker it would become. I finally reached the bottom, or what should have at least been the bottom anyway. I ordered Chorus to allow me to breathe underwater and to stop me from sinking. I then used my abilities to bend the water around me and to allow me to dip my head through the water.

It was a heart. Well, not a literal heart, that would be creepy. It was molten magma shaped like a heart. There were cylinders of magma circling their way to and from the heart and into the ground surrounding it. I looked at the water my body was in and the really hot space of air my head was in. It seemed the heat of the magma had evaporated all water in a close range of it, meaning the space of water I was in was like a small pond in a upside down bowl shaped world.

I then moved my head back into the water and swam away from the heart. I then saw a fish. No no. Not what you are thinking. It wasn't like a salmon or a shark or tuna, it was a massive salmon with multiple layers of shark teeth within its mouth. I thought about the basilisk I had fought and how this fish was nothing compared to a creature that could turn your body into stone.

I gulped down some water, which was somehow vaporised within my body to allow me to breathe. I used magical water jet propulsion to blast me forwards, sword pointed in front of me. Yeah, it really was as cool as it sounds.

A few easy going minutes later, I had used super strength (which Chorus bestowed upon me temporarily) to carry the massive dead fish from the depths and to the campfire.

"Make a spit!" I told my friends. Then they all spat on the floor in front of me. "No, I don't mean spit, I mean make a *spit*." Hurriedly, they collected some wood and brought out some rope that was in the tent and we made a makeshift campfire cooker. I then lifted up the fish and placed it on the spit. Using fire magic, I cooked the fish, the campfire below it serving no purpose, as I had realised.

"Ace, you know the fire—" Becky began.

"I know, I know," I said. I used Chorus to cut up the fish. My friends rapidly collected their plates, including my own, and I filled their plates with hearty servings of monster fish. We then settled down on the logs and ate the fish. It was a peculiar tasting. It had a salt and vinegar like taste and the texture of roast chicken. Sure it was nice, just very very different.

"Sad there's no fries to go with this." Jim sighed.

"All right, Mr England," I said. My friends laughed, I enjoyed myself and all was good, until I went to bed. Once I had settled down in my sleeping bag and settled off to sleep, I began to have very vivid dreams. It was a constant swirl of sickening green, with a huge fish swimming around me and the heart beating right next to my face.

I felt really hot on the right side of my face yet freezing cold on my left. I then turned to realise my left side was frozen within ice. I somehow laughed and began singing, but it wasn't my voice, it was Sulleth's voice. I felt like I was trapped within my own body. Suddenly, I saw Darf running around in circles, eating Becky while doing so, and I also saw Serpias eating all the others.

The swirling grew brighter and darker in a very nauseous way. My foot then threw up and everything turned upside down, then back right, then it all spun around. I then said, "Errm, what is happening." Which was kinda peculiar considering the fact that Sulleth was still singing a song, with two different voices coming out of my mouth.

I then snapped awake. I ran outside the tent and to the river and threw up again. It was serious deja vu from earlier that day. I had a few seconds of relief to see the other four throwing up to my side. I then continued to throw up into the river.

I woke up on the river bank, my friends to my side also waking up, coincidentally at the same time.

"Food poisoning?" I asked.

"Food poisoning," Libbie then replied with an answering tone. I just laid there on the snow.

"Haha!" Chorus laughed in its bracelet form.

"Wait…you KNEW the fish was poisonous," I demanded.

"Oh yes," sighed Chorus. "The poison won't kill you, it just makes you vastly sick."

"Why?" I asked with a helpless tone.

"What, you earthlings are the only ones that get to have fun, this is my fun," It replied.

"I thought that you were helpful, like a blessing," I said.

"That I am, yet sometimes us swords have to let out our emotions, of course, the good emotions." Chorus then continued to laugh.

"Bah," I said.

Chapter 18

It took us hours to prepare ourselves to go, Chorus mocking us all the time it took. We left the fish corpse in the water, to make sure no weary travellers or land animals had to go through what we did. We eventually made it back to the ice wall and back to our quest. The food poison had really thrown me off track and highly stressed me out.

Chorus had realised its mistake and was pleading forgiveness. "Ace, I am incredibly sorry for it. I had an idea to make a joke, that was all. I didn't mean for you to get upset like this." I ignored it. "Please, Ace, talk to me. It was a mere cause for a laugh. I meant not to frustrate you in such a way."

"I understand, yet you are one of the reasons I got stuck in this sucky quest, just so I could save *your* kingdom. I see no point in this," I replied. Suddenly, I was blasted back. I was laying on my back contemplating what had happened.

"How *dare* you insult Rimoor in such a way. If I must, I will find a new host. If you ever question the innocence of this kingdom again, I shall slay you," Chorus roared.

I then continued the conversation within my mind. "Chorus, you know I do not think of your kingdom like this. I want it to be safe as much as you, but realise that I do not belong here. My friends do not belong here. So how about you cut us some slack, like we had just been poisoned."

"I again apologise," said Chorus.

I then ended the conversation and said to my friends aloud, "It is all dealt with."

Much time had passed before I began to feel thirsty. I mean murderous thirst. I could tell my companions felt thirsty as well because they were actually moaning about how thirsty they were.

"Ace, can't you and Chorus do anything?" Jim said, almost crying.

"If Chorus cannot summon food, I don't think it can summon water," I replied. I was deeply regretting not stacking up on water at the river. "Is there any water nearby?" I asked Chorus.

"Are you guys acting dumb on purpose? There is water all around us," Chorus replied. I gave a puzzled look, but with nothing to direct it at, it must have just looked like I was staring off to the abyss. "Oh my, the *snow*," said Chorus. I instantaneously activated Chorus' sword form, set the blade alight and pointed it in front of us. Because of the vast calibre of the blizzard pounding the snow down on us, much water was already pouring off Chorus.

"GET THE FLASKS!" I shouted to the others, even though they were right next to me. Without hesitating, they brought their flasks out from under their winter coats and held it under Chorus. A few minutes later, we all had full flasks. I was gulping down so much water, I was afraid I would end up hurting myself.

"Oh god," Libbie mumbled.

"Yeah," I said. I don't know why I said *yeah*, it just seemed right at the time. We had begun walking again when I began wondering about how Cal was and if he was even still alive. Suddenly, my consciousness split into two. It was a very weird feeling. I could control my body and see what was happening through my eyes, yet what I believe was my soul was also existing in a separate area.

I saw a portly man of quite small size.

"CAL!" I shouted.

He flicked his head in fear. He was wearing slave's clothes of a plain white tunic and grey pants. He was enclosed within a tight space that forced him to curl up into a ball if he was to fit. Even though he was curled up, he was still very compressed, due to the fact that the Exelon empire probably made the spaces so small to purposely make it torturous for the slaves within them.

It was a metallic cocoon with a variation of metal pipes running through it. There were also holes in the space, roughly the size of a baby's fist. Emitting from Cal's body was a red smoke, which was sucked in by the holes. He turned his face towards me. He somehow could see my astral projection.

"Ace Ford?" Cal asked.

"Yeah, it's me," I replied.

"This is pure torture!" Cal cried. "The red stuff coming of me is my life force. Those holes are receivers that collect the force and turn it into energy, but they supply a small amount of energy to keep me alive, as to harvest the most of my life."

"Can you see anything?" I asked, as I could not see a thing.

"No, the chamber in which I am in has no windows, air vents, anything. The only reason that I can see is because my life force emits a sort of light, which I enjoy, even though it emits barely any light."

"Okay, we will free you, Cal, you will be open to the Rimoor sky anytime soon."

"I can sense that you have limited time left. Use the gift of Rince to free Rimoor, and kill Vex."

"I will," I said. Then my mind snapped back into one. I fell onto the ground, eyes wide open.

"Ace! Are you alright?" Austin said.

"I saw Cal," I replied. It was all I could manage.

"Okay, we will start walking again and you will tell us everything," Becky said. I could not put into words how ghastly the torture for Cal was. I merely mumbled as we were walking. I was making no words, simply senseless noises. After a while, I managed to tell them what I saw. Afterwards, upon their faces were the look of disgust.

"How could they!" Becky said. I didn't talk for a while, my head hung down in sadness. Thinking of the tortures of possibly hundreds of innocents, a rage filled within me. I then suddenly turned and walked towards the ice wall. Then I went into a frenzy of fury. I summoned Chorus and began slashing viciously at the wall. I couldn't tell how long I was there for, but it felt like just a few minutes when I had stopped.

I retracted Chorus back into its portable form while staring at the wall. Hundreds of slash marks scarred the ice wall. It surprised me how dark it was. It seemed to have become a much darker shade of grey. I turned around to see my friends sitting down on a log. No, not the campfire log, simply a log from a toppled tree.

"About time. We thought you'd never stop," said Jim. I felt as if I had lost so much anger that I felt like I could be ascending into the heavens right then.

"Yes. How long was I?" I asked.

"I don't fully know, possibly two hours," Libbie said. I could almost feel my eyes dilating. *Two hours*. I don't think that anyone had ever held a grudge for that long. "Excuse me!" I said, not specifically to my friends, more so to Chorus.

"Oh my, Ace, calm down. It was roughly two hours indeed, but if your wellbeing is positively heightened from the occurrence, then that is good," Chorus said.

"Oh, thanks for deafening me," Chorus said. "Another joke."

I was able to manage a laugh this time. "Let's get going," I said to the others.

Once they stood from the log and began walking, it became night. Literally, as soon as we had walked a few metres away from the log, it seemed to have become the dead of night. "Should we set up camp or…?" Austin asked.

"Let's walk for a bit more to make up for lost time," I replied. After what I suppose was an hour, we came across something…or someone. The blizzard and night was almost combining forces to make it as hard as possible for us to make it further north. Suddenly, we began to see a faint orange light peeking itself through the close cropped snow.

I picked up the pace, my friends following my example. The light began to brighten the nearer we walked towards it, as well as the light growing further outwards. I could sense that we were almost at the source of the light. Music began to play. It was the sound of a harp playing a low tune as well as a violin playing a soothing, yet strong song.

Out of the blizzard, I could see a fire pit, a circle of rocks with a blazing fire roaring upwards. There were also velvet sofas. Three large, red velvet sofas of a very exquisite design sat around the fire pit, the harp and the violin to the east of the set up. I noticed that the violin was levitating and playing by itself. The height of the violin was that of what a human would be if they were handling the musical instrument.

The harp sat upon the snow, the strings plucking themselves in a low gear, following the violin's melody. Much like the violin, the harp was playing by itself. Unlike stereotypical harps (being made of gold), it was made of silver. Sitting down upon one of the sofas, the one pointing to the ice wall, was a man. Yet, this person was very peculiar.

He wore black armour, and not a simple dark black like the robes Vex wore, but a black that seemed so dark that I could have thought that the man was 2D. White robes were wrapped around the man's armour. However, the person's helmet was the thing that caught my attention the most. It covered all of his head and his face, concealing his true appearance.

The helm was that of what I could only describe as a male Medusa. I don't believe that anywhere within the world I was in believed in Medusa, so it was a simple coincidence that I thought of the similarities between the two characters. The face was obviously that of a male, with a beard built into it and the shape of it being quite masculine.

Yet, the metallic face itself had no scars or marks, in fact, it was very smooth and clean. It would have been viewed as a feminine appearance of the time period which I supposed myself to be in. The thing that made me find the reference to Medusa was the hair. The metal hair built into it was shoulder length snakes, all coiling around the other and pointing to the direction where the face was pointing to.

He had no weapons of any kind showing themselves, so I guessed he must have had some hidden within his robes. He then turned his face away from the fire and towards us. It was unimaginably unsettling seeing such a realistic face watching you, emotionless, unblinking. And it didn't help that every time he turned his head, it looked like a 2D being changing its shape.

He then stood up and called out to us. "Greetings, please take a seat, we must converse!" Going against the man's appearance was his voice. It was a flattering, silky voice that would be perfectly used by a person who used their voice to deceive very often. I walked towards the sofa next to the one the being was in, Libbie sat next to me and the other three sitting together. The man sat down upon his own sofa.

"Who are you?" I ventured.

"I am the one that shall help you through parts of your struggles," said the mystery man. "I sense a feeling of distrust within you."

"Why would I feel trustful? There randomly is a set of sofas, a fire pit, and music just sitting along our travels north."

"It is no coincidence," said the being.

"Clearly," I replied. My friends were deadly silent, still taking in the person's peculiar clothing, particularly the helmet.

"Ha, you feel uncomfortable with my helm, I can tell. It is purposefully built in such a way to scare my enemies before I slay them. I also can tell you are not from here. You think I look similar to a monster within a mythology that beings from this realm do not believe in."

"How can you tell?" I countered.

"Magic. It can work wonders, yet it can also destroy faith in life," said the man. He reached into his robes and pulled out a dagger. He did not wield it in any offensive way but he simply rolled it through his fingers in a playful fashion.

"Specifically, why are you here?" Libbie finally said, breaking my friend's silence.

"Heed my warning, a town is ten miles north. It is Exelon ruled but not as protected as the town you have seen beforehand."

"Why do you warn us now and not before we reached the highly protected town we had recently come across?" I asked.

"Because this town has a carriage system that directly takes you to Chalin fortress. I believe it could be of use to you. Again, I cannot directly interfere with your quest but I can point you in the right direction," the person replied.

"As a connection to before, why should we trust you?" Austin said.

"Because I also have a hatred towards the empire as well," the man said.

"You could be lying to us," I said.

"Just as easily as I could be telling you the truth," the being said, still keeping their cool. "Believe it or not, the Exelon empire has stopped my attempts to slay Serpias. With the ice borders, I cannot march a legion in here to kill her."

"You know of Serpias?" I questioned.

"Indeed, I know of her kind very well."

"This is a change of subject! Tell us what you think we must do once we reach the next town," Libbie snapped.

"Haha! A feisty one. I can tell you, or should I not." Libbie's eyes narrowed. "I am simply teasing you!" The man said.

"I would prefer not to be teased at this moment in time," said Libbie savagely.

"Ahh. Alright. I suggest that once you reach the town, you stock up on supplies and stay at an inn. You seem as if you need a proper bed. Once you have done that, take a carriage to Chalin fortress, there is a stopping point in between the fortress and the town, exit the carriage there and walk the rest of the way. You must then sneak into the fortress and make your way out of it. You cannot stay in the carriage, otherwise you will die," warned the man.

"I must now take my leave." Suddenly, the music stopped and the fire went out. The man stood from his sofa. Like Count Charles' guards, the instruments and firepit sank into the dark ground. Then the sofas followed the other objects' lead. Each of the three sofas sank into the dark ground with me and my friends on sofas. Once they had breached the solid ground, me and my companions were lying on our backs.

"WHAT IS YOUR NAME?" I shouted to the man. Without responding, he, like the rest of the zone, sank quickly into the shadowed ground, not to be seen. Then I blanked out. It was a dreamless sleep. I awoke at the same time as the rest of my friends. I stood. It was now day time.

I asked Chorus, "Who was that man?"

Chorus then replied saying, "For the first time, my magic has failed me. I cannot recognise the man. He truly is of a mysterious factor that beats even the likes of god-like magic."

"Hmmm," I mumbled.

"He was right though, when you were asleep, I took the time to identify what the being had said. By the looks of it, there actually *is* a town ten miles north from here with a carriage system that leads to the fortress."

I pulled out my flask and gulped down a load of water. "Okay, guys, let's get to that town," I said. My friends started to get up and following me.

Chapter 19

"So, that man was quite, errm, weird," Libbie said to me. I was quite startled as I was thinking much about the man myself.

"I know, he gave me some sort of vibes that we should not be working with him," I replied.

"Working? We won't be working with the guy, sure we can listen to what he said but we will *definitely* not work with him," Libbie said.

"Alright, jeez," I replied.

"Jeez, really. How mature." Libbie sighed before walking back to Becky.

"Ayy, Chorus," I said.

"Never heard that before, but I'll take it. Hi, Ace," Chorus said humorously.

"So, I have been hearing a lot about this world because of you and, personally, I would like to know about Rimoor's history itself," I said.

"Oh, nobody has ever actually asked me that before. Okay, so Rimoor is a kingdom within the continent of Kevener. Now, Kevener goes by many different names within the different kingdoms that reside in it, but the most well-known name for it is Kevener. So Rimoor's usual climate is what you Earthling humans call Mediterranean."

"Rimoor is full of culture revolving around equality and fairness, which the royal family of Rimoor implement. We all have jobs within the community that help each other. Also, Rimoor is one of the most magically connected kingdoms in Kevener, meaning we do have a strong military and trade routes, but we don't ever really use the military as this kingdom is quite peaceful."

"Peace was within this kingdom for many centuries before the Exelon cult was founded by Sulleth and an offspring branch of the Knights of Eternalis Brotherhood—"

I then cut Chorus of. "Wait! The people that hunted down Serpias' species helped raise the Exelon cult to power?"

"Indeed. Sulleth somehow manipulated the Brotherhood into helping him start his cult."

"Well, that is very disturbing," I mumbled.

Chorus then sighed. "I don't wish to tell you any more about Rimoor's history. It is making me nostalgic to the simpler past."

"Okay, I understand," I said. Chorus then fell silent.

Ideas flooded my mind. If Sulleth could manipulate an entire branch of a powerful brotherhood to his side, who knows what else he could do. It was making me wonder if Vex would actually be the one who failed in what I believe to be a secretive tactic to use the other (when I say other, I mean Sulleth and Vex).

"Ace, you seem depressed," Jim said, running up to me. I hadn't realised but my face had become scrunched up in a very unflattering way.

"Oh, I'm not, I'm just wondering," I said.

"About what?" Jim replied asking.

"Just about…" I thought about how Chorus would blow up like a nuclear bomb if I lied. "The origins of Rimoor," I finished.

Jim then shrugged. "Do you think we will ever get out of here?" He asked.

"Ehh, always the possibility," said Becky, having stepped back to talk with us.

"Don't think about it in a negative way such as that. We have to stay positive," I said.

"Stay positive." Becky snorted with laughter. "I could be positive, but that ruins the fun about being negative."

"Are you being sarcastic?" Jim asked Becky.

"No, I defo ain't being sarcastic," said Becky…sarcastically.

"You are now confusing me more than the time Davy Smiths accidentally turded himself while in the dinner hall, then emptied it onto a roast dinner plate and swapped it with someone else's, and when that someone ate it, he didn't notice," Jim continued.

"Or when Stacy Driver went to the bathroom and accidentally peed in the sink," Becky said.

"Oh glorious, orphanage stories!" I said. Some really messed up stuff happened at the orphanage.

"How about when carer Platownski bullied Barny Towler for always wearing a bow tie," Jim countered. I had never understood that story. One of the carers whose job was to educate us in not bullying, ended up bullying.

"However, there was that time those eight year olds wanted to get married and the carers actually brought in an entire ceremony," Becky said, shivering. "Messed up prank the carers pulled there."

We just thought about other stories. It was helping us make our way through the blizzard. "Remember when I accidentally jumped off my bike and into that ditch," I said.

"Alright, we came to the conclusion that you did it on purpose because you were attention-seeking," Becky said.

"How rude," I mumbled, but it was the truth though. We ended up laughing it all off.

We finally came across the town that would lead us to Chalin fortress. However, it was already beginning to darken by the time we reached the first house. It did not have huge walls and Exelon banners like Count Charles' town did, so I guessed it had to be more of a laid back town. It was a simplistic Rimoor town, with wooded and sometimes stone houses, with stables and bars.

It had a couple of market places and a few inns. We had finally reached the town square when it was full night time. "Guys, an inn!" Austin said. We looked towards where he was pointing, which was hard because of the blizzard, but when we did see what he was pointing at we saw a stone inn with the sign 'Inn' hanging above the entrance.

I am aware that we had passed many inns already, but this inn was slap bang in town square, so it was the best choice. Once we entered, I felt a feeling of relief. The constant assault of the blizzard was not slaughtering my face and open skin. It was dry and warm.

A balding fat man was sitting at the desk, opposite the entrance. The hair he still had was a light greyish. He was wearing a white tunic and blue overalls.

"Hello," I said, after we reached the desk.

"Ai," the man replied, looking at my face.

"Uhhm, do you have any rooms available?"

"Ai," said the man again.

"Oooookay," I replied, pulling out three silver coins. They were the ones that I had picked up many weeks ago at Cal's cabin. "Will these do for a night?" I asked.

"It is just for the five of ya?" The guy replied asking.

"Yes."

"Ai, that will do. See dat amount of coin can get ya a free bar pass," he said.

"Alright," I replied.

I passed the man the three silver coins, him giving me a key in exchange. "Second floor, fifth door to da left," he finalised. "Ya have a good stay."

Me and my friends then walked over to a staircase to the right of the man. We began our climb. Once we reached the second floor, we walked down the hallway and found our room. I unlocked the room and entered, my friends right behind me. Jim came in last so he shut the door. There were two bunk beds and one double bed.

"I call the single bed!" Libbie shouted. I noticed a door opposite the closest of the bunk beds. I walked over to it and opened it. Somehow an entire bar was situated in the door. I became aware that another room was meant to be right through the wall opposite the bunk beds, so I knew it had to be magic.

I stepped in and walked to the bar. I took a seat on a rickety wooden stool.

"What is there?" I asked.

The man at the bar jerked his head up without answering. I looked above the bar and saw a list of drinks. Only alcohol was available though.

"Do you know only alcohol is served here?" I asked the man.

"Yes, so?" The barkeep replied. Suddenly, I realised there were no age restrictions for drinks. My friends then entered, taking a place at the bar next to me.

"We can get any drink here," I whispered to Austin.

"So what will it be for you all?" The barkeep asked.

"Give us a large bottle of your strongest mead," I said.

"Ace, I don't think we have the money," Libbie said to me.

"Remember what the man at the till said, we get free drinks," I replied. I know, I know. We were on a quest and we shouldn't have been drinking, but we needed to relax, so one tiny drink couldn't hurt right?

Wrong! Ever so wrong! The next thing I remember was dancing with a tankard of what the barkeep called Runchard mead in my grasp. Roughly forty new people had entered the bar from their own designated doors dotted around the bar. A band had also entered, playing some sort of folk song on a podium. Twenty of the people in the bar were also dancing with me.

I was hosting a very giddy feeling that nothing in the world could hurt me. It felt amazing. I then took a huge gulp of my Runchard mead and walked back to the bar where Libbie and Becky were conversing. Jim and Austin were nowhere to be seen, probably socialising with the locals. I sat down on the stool and picked up the bottle of mead. I poured another tankard full into my…well, tankard.

"More!" I roared, as I noticed we had finished our third bottle of mead. The barkeep ran to a mead cabinet and pulled out a new bottle.

He walked over to me and said, "This bottle is traditional Rimoorian mead. It has a sweeter taste."

"Okay, that sounds good," I mumbled as I grabbed the bottle, uncorked it, drank the rest of the mead that was in my tankard and filled it up with the new mead.

I took a small sip. "Hmmm, that is very nice!" I said. It indeed was sweeter.

"Y'all seem not from round 'ere," the barkeep told me.

"Oh, just, we are people who are trying to remap all of Rimoor." I came up with it.

"Y'all seem a bit too young to be mappers."

"We all have a growth disorder," I replied.

"Gah, enjoy your night," the barkeep said before walking off and serving other people. I grabbed my tankard tighter and walked off into the crowd. I took a large swig before seeing Jim lounging on a couch, talking to these people in Exelon robes.

Chapter 20

I was freaking out. It was definitely people of the empire because they were wearing Exelon robes. The robes looked much like the Earth's Ku Klux Klan robes and hood, but the colouring of the robes were a dark crimson with the Exelon symbol stitched to the front hand back of the robes. I walked closer, pushing Chorus' bracelet form higher up my wrist, as to hide it with my sleeve.

"Hey, Jim!" I said to Jim in a very annoyed tone. "Can I talk with you for a moment?"

"Sure." Jim then rose from the sofa and walked to me. Because of the band and the people talking, we didn't have to walk far before being out of earshot of the Exelon robes people.

"Why are you talking to them?" I asked furiously.

"Well, I saw them and I began talking with them," Jim replied with a simplistic tone.

"Okay, this is very important, did you tell them anything about the quest?"

"Oh god, no! Sure, I think I may be a little drunk but I would never actively talk to the enemies about the quest," Jim said. A wave of relief settled over me. Then Jim snatched my tankard and took a large gulp.

"Alright, let's head back to them and end that conversation," I told Jim. We approached the robed people. "This is Brenard," Jim said pointing to me. I already became aware that he was going to come up with a story.

"Yep, that's me, I'm Brenard." I laughed nervously.

"Well, Brenard, Jim, come sit with us," said one of the robed people. It was that of a woman's voice. We sat down.

"Don't be nervous. We may be an elite mortal force, but we will not hurt you," said another. That voice was that of a man.

"Oh, we aren't nervous, just…" I began. I couldn't come up with a finish to the sentence. There were three of the Exelon people.

"HAHA! There is no shame in being nervous!" The last one boomed. It was also that of a woman.

"Alright," I mumbled.

"So, you have heard so much about me, let's hear about *you*," said Jim to the people.

"Fine. I am Captain Aria, I lead this squadron of three. This one next to me is William and the one standing, she is Gurt," said the first person who spoke.

"We are the, ahh, witches of Sulleth's coven," said the man whose name was William.

I gulped nervously. "Coven?" I asked.

"It is a group of witches," said Aria. "Sulleth was an old person of significance to the empire, and our squadron is a coven whose entire purpose is to impose the original wishes of Lord Sulleth."

"We answer only to Lord Vex," boomed Gurt. "Of course Lord Sulleth is dead, so we believe that we are the only true enforcers of what Sulleth would truly have wanted to have become of the empire," Aria continued.

"Very interesting," Jim said.

I had become very aware that the witches who said they were the only ones to enforce Sulleth's original wants didn't actually know that Sulleth was still alive.

Well, not really alive-alive, but more so undead-alive.

Bah! Too complicated!

"So, can you do magic?" I asked.

"Indeed, but all three of us specialise in different types of magic," William continued.

"William is speaking the truth," Aria said. "I specialise more in active attack spells, such as elemental manipulation, while William specialises in rituals and Gurt...well, she specialises in weapon magic."

"They speak truth, I can summon weapons," grunted Gurt.

"Is Gurt human?" I whispered to Aria.

She let out a hearty laugh. "She is a quarter-giantess!" Aria chuckled.

Only a quarter! She was enormous, roughly twice the size of a fully grown man.

"Oh god," I mumbled.

"Well, human blood filters down the size," Aria said. I nearly threw up. How big were proper giants!

"Ha! You fear me!" Gurt laughed with a very low pitched voice.

I really wanted to shout *YOU THINK!* but I mentally held myself back. I didn't want to show weakness to the enemy. "Fear is a way of life." William shrugged.

"Yeah, so we must be off now, we have to get back to our friends," I said.

"Ahh, understandable. But before you go, take this," Aria said before pulling a scroll out of her robes, the scroll being shut by a wax seal. I took it. "Just to make sure you children don't get kidnapped while in your sleep," Aria said.

Me and Jim then stood. "Well, see you," Jim said, before we speed walked away from them and towards our friends. We weaved our way through the crowd, until we reached the bar and to Becky and Libbie. Austin had re-joined them.

"What's wrong?" Libbie asked, seeing the worried looks on mine and Jim's faces.

"We have to get out of the bar and lock the door!" I said to them, in a decently quiet but very serious tone.

"Why?" Austin asked.

"Exelon people," I said in a more rapid way. My friend's eyes widened in terror.

"Really?" Libbie asked urgently.

"Yes, so hurry."

Austin, Becky, and Libbie then went on to stand up and follow me to the doorway we entered from. Once all five of us entered, I shut the door and found a key. I tried to see if the key would fit into the keyhole in the door, and it did. I locked the door and sat down on one of the lower bunk beds. I was breathing heavily. Fear was coursing through my veins.

"That was awfully close," said Becky.

"Yeah, better stay low for the rest of the night," Jim said.

I was mentally running through what could have happened. One: they were lying and knew who we actually were. Two: they were lying about themselves and were a wannabe group. This trail of thought went on for quite some time. When I finally snapped out of this trance-like state, I realised that the candles were out and my friends were sleeping.

"What in the name of god happened?" I asked Chorus mentally.

"Well, you were thinking, and they went to sleep," Chorus replied, again mentally.

"Alright, I can cope with that, but who *were* those people?" I said.

"Who?"

"The people in Exelon robes."

"Ahh, yes, they were all that they said they were, but they don't actually know of Sulleth still existing," Chorus answered.

"Oh great, we are in the same inn as the enemies," I mumbled. I then laid down and fell asleep.

I awoke the next morning with a very, very, unimaginably painful headache.

"Owwww!" I mumbled, as I began to sit up in bed. I could see my friends all laying on the floor or on their beds moaning in pain. "Why did we drink so much!" Jim shouted.

"I don't know!" Becky shouted back, with no apparent reason.

"How long have you guys been like this?" I mumbled loudly.

"At least forever," cried Jim. We just stayed where we were. It went on for Rince knows how long.

After what felt like two hours, I sat up. "Okay, I'm feeling better."

"Yes, so am I," said Libbie, beginning to stand up. Once we all stood up, claiming to be feeling better, we began to walk out of the room into the hallway. Within a period of a few minutes, we had walked down the stairs and found what seemed to be a cafe. It was a conjoined room, connected to the entrance room. Once we had sat down, we looked at the menu. It all seemed very…foreign.

Of course it is, you are in a different world for god's sake! I said to myself in my mind. Then a woman in silver clothes walked up to me and my friend's table.

"Order?" She asked in a very polite tone.

"Err, could I please have…" I said, looking back at the menu. There were no pictures of the meal so I had to take a hopeful guess. "The Travilan caw with some spiced beans and some Aavial talls sausage."

"Okay, and for the rest of you?" She asked.

"What do you guys want?" Libbie asked the other three. They all shrugged. Libbie sighed before replying, "We'll all have the same."

"Okay, will that be all?" The woman asked finally.

"Yes," I replied. The woman then walked off to a doorway which I believe led to the kitchen. I looked around the cafe and saw three specific people sitting around a table. They were the members of the witches of Sulleth's coven. They were wearing the same robes, but this time without the weirdly shaped hoods.

I could clearly see two women and one man. The smaller of the two women, the one named Aria, had auburn coloured hair and green eyes. The man named William had no hair and hazel eyes, while the quarter-giantess named Gurt had long, greasy black hair with quite a few black beard hairs producing from her face. She had orange eyes and pupils like that of a cat, and of course, she was twice the size of a fully grown man.

160

Gurt took up half of the table and had to sit on two chairs, which were wobbling and threatening to break under Gurt's weight. A shiver ran through my spine. Out of all the three witches, Gurt definitely scared me the most. I looked away and back to my friends.

"They are here," I said.

"Who?" Austin said.

"The enemies we came across last night. The witches of Sulleth's coven," I answered.

"Where!" Jim shouted.

"Don't shout and definitely don't look for them, we have to seem unaffected by them being here," I hissed.

"O-okay," mumbled Jim. Nervousness echoed through all five of us. After another ten, possibly twenty minutes, our food came.

"Is this for you?" The same woman who took our orders asked.

"Yes," said Libbie, taking her plate, the rest of us claiming our own plates.

The woman then walked off. For definite, the meal wasn't what I was expecting. There was a large slab of sickly green meat and the sausages were white. The beans looked like Earthly baked beans, except the beans on my plate had some spices mixed into it. "This looks… weird," Austin mumbled.

I took the risk for all of us and had a mouthful of the beans. Even though the thought of spiced beans sounded absolutely revolting, it actually tasted quite nice, with a tangy aftertaste. I then tried the slab of meat. It had its own taste and texture. It was easy to cut yet hard to chew, and it tasted like someone had mixed some roast beef and lamb together, then injected gravy into it. In other words, it was delicious.

Becky then tried the sausage. Her eyes suddenly rolled up into her head in ecstasy.

"It may look weird but it is so good!" Becky said to the others.

One by one, the other three began to eat their meals. While we were eating, I constantly hastened glances at the witches, just in case they noticed us. After we had finished, we simply sat in silence. Finally, Libbie broke the silence saying, "Christ, that was good."

The others then burst into conversation but I was distracted. I saw the three members of the squadron walk towards us.

"Brenard!" Aria burst out saying.

"Hi," I said in return. A look of confusion settled over Austin, Libbie, and Becky. I then went on to glare at them, in what seemed to be a menacing way. They got the idea.

"Oh, hi," said Libbie.

"Good morrow! May the day bring much prosperity for the empire!" William said.

"Indeed," replied Jim.

"We came to say goodbye as we were going to head off now. Emperor Vex has demanded us to hunt down these so-called 'Liberators of Rimoor'. Idiotic right?" Aria said.

"Yes, definitely," Becky said.

Gurt then sniffed the air. Another shiver travelled down my spine. I felt as if she knew something that the other two did not.

"Well bye," I said, hoping that they would leave quickly. As I said bye, the witches walked out of the cafe. The last thing I saw of them were them flicking their wrists, their hoods materialising out of thin air onto their heads.

"Oh lord almighty!" I said. I let out a long sigh.

"That was very stressful," said Libbie. I then called one of the waiters over and asked for a glass of water.

"Oh yeah, one for me too," said Austin.

"And me," said Becky. After almost a second, Jim and Libbie had also asked for a glass. Ever...so...close...

Once we had drunk our water and had our water flasks filled, we began to prepare to leave.

"I really want to stay another night," moaned Jim.

"We can't, destiny awaits us," Libbie replied.

"Alright, all of us ready?" I asked. They all replied 'yes'. "Okay, let's get going then!" I said, before stepping out of the inn.

A sudden blast of cold hit me. The familiar feeling of the snow assaulting my face began their attack once again. I looked around the town square. The streets were bustled with people, carriages travelling along the cobblestone road. I remembered the way we came, so I began walking in the opposite direction.

Somehow, the snow had become thicker but in weaker amounts, meaning I could see the town square quite clearly. I weaved in and out of the people, my four friends close behind me. We passed more tea shops and marketplaces but I forced myself not to pay attention to such things. Before I knew it, we had left the town and were out into the wilderness.

I looked around and saw a carriage, roughly twice the size of a regular one, settled down on a patch of stone, being piled up with weapons, armour, livestock, and much more. I knew that the carriage had to be the one that would take us to Chalin fortress.

"Guys, follow me," I told the other four.

I began to sneak towards the carriage. Luckily, the driver and the people filling up the carriage didn't notice us. The horses that were harnessed to the carriage were beautiful brown and roughly, like the carriage, twice the size of a regular horse. While all the people who were filling up the carriage were looking away, me, Becky, Libbie, Jim and Austin all jumped into the carriage and behind a stack of crates, as to be hidden by the people filling up the carriage.

After a minute or two, we began to move. It was quite wobbly, being on a cobblestone road (as there was a road that led out of the town and up north). Somehow, none of the crates fell upon us. The livestock were mainly silver chickens, purple pigs, and a variety of smaller animals. As we were wobbling down the road, I sat down upon the wooden floor of the carriage and relaxed. Who knows when the next time I would get to relax would be.

I looked around the carriage and saw axes, hammers, swords, fruits, and vegetables. But one specific thing caught my attention: an extremely large crate labelled 'Sensitive'. I pulled my thoughts away from the crate and looked towards my friends, who like me, had sat down on the floor.

"Can you believe it?" Jim asked.

"Believe what?" Austin replied.

"That we have travelled this far," said Jim.

"Yes, but it does feel quite unsettling knowing that we still have a while of travelling to do," Libbie said.

"Damn, I can't take this any longer," I said, before standing up and walking towards the 'sensitive' crate. I put my left ear against the wooden crate. I heard breathing. "Guys, something is in here," I mumbled.

"What is it?" Libbie asked.

"I don't know but it is definitely something alive." Then the being within the crate let out a loud screech.

"Shut it back there, Barthemalue!" The driver shouted. I stumbled back.

"Whatever is in there, it definitely wants to get out," I whispered, as to not attract attention to the driver.

"This is really suspicious," said Becky. "I think this is not what we think it is."

"Really, I have a feeling that this is exactly what we think it is," I replied.

After what I believed to be half-a-hour, the carriage suddenly slowed and stopped.

"Okay, gotta make sure nothin' fell out," I heard the driver say. I then heard the sound of someone jumping into the snow, the sound of crunching footsteps afterwards.

"Guys, let's go," whispered Libbie. We then stood and began sneaking out of the carriage and around to its right side. Luckily, the driver had been walking around the left side of the carriage.

"Run," Libbie said to us.

We then ran past the carriage and the horses, heading further north. I heard no shouting behind us, so I claimed that the carriage driver hadn't noticed us. After roughly another ten minutes had passed, we all stopped. I went through my breathing exercises. The carriage was nowhere in sight. Had we outrun it?

"Chorus, h-how much more f-f-further until we reach the fortress," I mumbled.

Chorus then replied saying, "Oh, well, do you really want to know?"

"Yes, why else would I have asked."

"Alright, but I really don't think you want to hear this."

"Come one, just tell me."

"Well, it's right there."

Chapter 21

It wasn't exactly 'Right there' but it was in plain sight, roughly a quarter of a mile away. It somehow split the amount of snow being produced. I could see a huge arch protruding from the ice wall, connecting to the main body of the fortress. The fortress was made of white concrete and marble.

The pathway the carriage was travelling across swerved and passed through the archway connecting the fortress and the ice wall. Zombie warriors were marching around the fortress walls and the perimeter of the stronghold. It was roughly ten stories tall with a mixture of small and enormous windows.

"Oh god…" screamed Libbie.

"How big is that!" Becky shouted.

The roof of the fortress consisted of one large dome and a vaulted ceiling. Suddenly, anxiety pulsed through my veins. Out of nowhere the carriage we had hid in passed us on the road and followed it along until it reached the arch, where it stopped. A group of zombie warriors marched up to the carriage.

They entered it and began hauling the contents of the carriage out, passing it to slaves who carried it into the fortress. "Oh my," I whispered to myself. It was so large it could easily have been a royal palace.

"Why are we standing around?" Chorus asked.

"Just, fear I suppose," Austin mumbled.

"Well, this stronghold is nothing in size compared to the Capital Land Temple of Obsidian. Think about that and let's get moving, as the worst is yet to come," Chorus said.

"Alright," replied Austin.

We began walking towards the fortress. Fear. Such deep fear. I never would have thought that we would have made it so far. I stopped in my tracks. I saw a cave entrance to my right. I changed direction and marched towards the cave. Completely sure that the cave I was walking to was the cave that I saw Serpias and Darf in within one of my previous visions, I prepared myself for anything.

Once I had entered, I examined the cave. It was medium sized and empty. There were no signs of Darf or Serpias ever being there. I heard the other four arriving at the entrance to the cave just as I heard a yell above me. I looked up to see Darf dropping from the cave roof. He landed on me.

Sprawling on the floor, I pushed Darf away from me and rolled to safety. I stood and summoned Chorus.

"S-s-serpias is g-gone," said Darf. "Before sh-she left, she told m-m-me to a-await you here." Ever so quickly, Darf charged at me. I sidestepped, dodging Darf. I raised Chorus.

"We could help you!" I said to Darf. "Would you like that?"

Darf's eyes suddenly widened. "I-I would b-b-but it is to l-late for me. My t-town has been destroyed. There is no future f-f-for me." Darf then waddled forwards in a very unmenacing way. "I wish not t-to exist in a w-w-w-world

168

where I serve n-no purpose. As a l-last wish, please end this misery."

"If it is what you want, but are you sure?" I asked.

"D-d-definitely," said Darf.

"Alright, goodbye, Darf," I finalised before pulling back my sword and jabbing Chorus within Darf's heart. Darf then fell back, a silver smoke issuing from his mouth.

Then in a calm, smooth voice, one much like Darf's except calmer, the smoke said, "Thank you."

I changed Chorus back into its bracelet form. "We gotta go now," I said to the others. I looked towards them. They all nodded hurriedly. Walking back outside the cave, my friends right behind me, I began walking towards the fortress.

Within five minutes, I ducked down and began crawling on my stomach towards the fortress. I then noticed my friends doing the same thing. I saw a zombie warrior patrolling along the side of the stronghold's walls. I stood quickly, summoning my blade as I rose, making it turn into a blazing sword before stabbing the zombie warrior within its heart. It then toppled.

I looked towards the oak door. It wasn't the main entrance as the main entrance was heavily guarded by golem warriors, causing me to decide to enter using a side door. I walked towards the door, hand on handle before slowly opening it. I peeked my head in. I noticed that the hallway was empty, so I opened the door further and crept in. My friends were also with me, also sneaking into Chalin fortress.

With Chorus in hand, and my friends (except for Libbie who was wielding her new war-hammer) who had their harpes unsheathed, we walked along the corridor, waiting for something, anything to occur. We came to a junction. I decided to turn left, as to head deeper into the fortress. We then came across a zombie warrior. I then, with my sword ablaze, slayed the undead soldier.

"Why are we going further into the fortress?" Becky whispered.

"More possible exits," I replied quietly. Turning more corners, we then came across an atrium. It had glass skylights with many chandeliers hanging across the glass. There was a large staircase leading to a second floor of the fortress. Unsurprisingly (because of the size of the fortress), there were no beings, dead or alive, anywhere in sight.

I then decided to head to the second floor because of the chance to find…well anything really. As we climbed the stairs, I heard the talking of a zombie warrior. "You don't really think they could make it this far?" I froze in place.

"Well, there is always the possibility, we must stay open minded and use our own free will, the last we have of it, to think of what *if*," said a second.

"True. But they really couldn't. First, they would have to survive the blizzard alone, pass through Exelon ruled towns and sneak into this very fortress. It is very improbable of them reaching the northern ice wall without either being imprisoned or being caught," replied the first.

"Bah! You and your thoughts!"

I then heard them walking towards the staircase I was standing on.

"Get down quick!" I whispered urgently to the others. We hurriedly tiptoed down the stairs and around to the side of the staircase. We stood there until I saw the two zombie warriors finally walk down the last step and the corridor that led out of the atrium. I then, without speaking, walked around the staircase and walked back to the top of it.

"That was awfully close," said Jim who, like the others, had sneaked up the staircase and stepped next to me.

"I know," I replied quietly.

We quickly walked down multiple corridors and through empty rooms. I then heard a laugh. I ran around the next corner and plunged my newly ablaze blade into the gut of a zombie warrior. I then removed Chorus from the zombie and carried on my venture through Chalin fortress.

"Are we near an exit?" I whispered to Chorus.

"I am not sure, the power of the fortress is interfering with my navigation system," Chorus replied.

"Great," I whispered. We were lost within an enormous enemy base. I took my mind away from the subject. I carried on sneaking through the stronghold, hiding behind the occasional door or wall and often slaying an undead enemy. After a period of ten minutes, we were completely lost and a zombie was usually around every single corner.

Then the thing of nightmares occurred. A cold hand gripped my shoulder. I turned around to see an armoured zombie looking down at me with empty eye sockets.

"Damn…" I mumbled. "So close."

Six other warriors were standing, grasping my friends in their undead grip. We were then escorted through a vast series of rooms and corridors, and up many flights of stairs. Eventually, we came across double birch, iron wrought doors. Two of the seven zombie warriors marched forwards and pushed the doors open. We were then pushed inside.

I heard the doors slam closed behind me. We were then taken down an exquisitely decorated room by the remaining five warriors. The room itself was beautiful. It had a red velvet carpet leading from the double entrance doors to a podium.

The podium had steps leading up it. Then, three metres away, on either side of the carpet, were marble pillars leading to a vaulted ceiling. Behind the pillars were golden walls.

I do not mean gold painted walls, I mean the walls were literally made out of solid gold. There were enormous windows along the walls to the left and right of me, and the floor was made of a greyish marble. Finally, we stopped at the bottom of the podium. Upon the elevated flooring was a pure black throne, which did not suit the overall theme of the room at all.

But upon the throne… "Greetings! I am Governor Frederick! However, you peasants may know me as Frederick, the Vicious. I am the governor of this glorious stronghold, Chalin fortress. Attempt to manipulate me, I suggest you do not do, as I already know who you pathetic children are. You are the saviours of Rimoor!" The governor let out a hearty laugh.

He had shoulder length, curly blonde hair and a long blonde beard. His eyes were the deepest of maroon. He was also ever so pale. His appearance was much like the likes of Vex, except he had different coloured eyes and hair, and also wasn't as thin. He was wearing golden armour which covered all of his body except for his head. Yes, it also covered his hands.

Over the armour were sleeveless, green robes that fell to his feet. At his waist hung a peculiar sword. It had the blade of a greatsword, except it was curved. It had a golden epee bell guard and a curved hilt. Very weird. To his left were three very specific figures.

"Greetings, Ace," said William. It was the witches of Sulleth's coven! William had his pointed hood up to hide his face and head, but Gurt and Aria had their hoods off, revealing their heads and faces.

"Oh, are you actually kidding me!" I shouted.

"Well, you were not expecting that, were you, Ace?" Frederick, the Vicious said. But to the right of Frederick was a robed being. I could not tell any features. The being was shrouded in torn, black robes that covered all of its body. Its head was also in a black hood, obscuring the beings face from view. It was a very unsettling sight.

I could not see its chest rising or falling, meaning it was not breathing, and it was standing still. I mean still, not moving at all. It didn't sway or breathe or shuffle. It was as still as a statue. I teared my eyes off the figure and looked towards the governor.

"I don't want to hurt anyone here," Libbie said.

"Hmm? Is that really the truth?" Frederick asked. Libbie did not answer.

"All we want to do is go home, and the only way to do that is to complete this quest!" I snapped.

"Are you sure?" Frederick replied coolly. I hadn't thought about that. Was it possible that If I died, I would awaken on the beach where all of this began?

"Aha," laughed Frederick. "You are not sure! It seems that your sword cannot answer all of your questions for you." He then gestured towards my right arm. I looked at it. Chorus wasn't in my grasp! Instead, I had Chorus in bracelet form wrapped around my wrist.

I hadn't ordered Chorus to transform. Was it possible that Chorus was so afraid, it sank back into its smaller form by itself.

"His weapon is afraid," mocked Aria.

"Ha!" Gurt said. It was not a laugh, she literally said the word.

"You seem, ahh, very annoyed," said Frederick.

"Of course I am," I replied.

"And why is that?" Frederick pushed. I did not reply. "I honestly judge you and your little quest. I find it unneeded. The empire holds Rimoor in capable and strong hands."

"Why should we believe you?" Jim asked.

"Because you only hear one side of the story," Frederick replied.

"I have *seen* plenty enough to say otherwise," I muttered.

"Very testy, aren't you? I cannot tell you how much I would like to kill you five filth, but Lord Vex has ordered me not to. I am quite irritated because of this. Has anyone told you people that you children have awfully infant-like faces." The governor laughed. We stayed silent.

"Now, I have explicit orders not to kill you, but I have no orders against torturing you. Captain Aria, do as you please." Aria then pushed her hands forwards in a shove-like motion. A crushing pain in my chest occurred. I knelt down onto my knees grasping my chest, hoping that the feeling would end. It didn't.

"They are not trying to fight off my spell," said Aria, the witch.

"Haha! Kneel! Kneel you feeble children. Bow and obey! Suffer the likes of torture!" Frederick laughed.

"Chorus…help!" I said to myself, hoping Chorus would respond.

"I-I cannot. I feel like I am incapable," Chorus cried.

"You are not!" I shouted in return. "You are literally a god sword!"

174

"He thinks his blade can counter the likes of your magic." William chuckled, speaking to Aria. Frederick continued his ruthless laughter at the sight of me and my friends being tortured.

"I have practised magic for decades now, Ace. You cannot beat me," said Aria.

"I m-may not be able to," I breathed. "But there is always a chance." A sudden wave of power and energy rushed through me. I stood up, Chorus elongating into my hand. Using the magic of Chorus, I snapped the magical bonds Aria was using to bring us pain.

I set Chorus alight and stabbed the zombie warrior next to me, then the others. I extinguished Chorus while freeing my friends from the curse.

"That is not possible!" Aria roared.

Governor Frederick chuckled in glee. "Maybe I might actually get to see you die."

"Very unlikely." I laughed.

"Oi!" Gurt shouted. I turned my head towards her. Then one of the most sickening, disgusting, mind-scarring things happened. Gurt flared her nostrils and her nose hairs extended from her nose, wrapping around each other to form tentacles of nose hair. I nearly threw up. Even though it took roughly a hundred hairs to make up a single tentacle, thirteen tentacles produced from her nostrils, seven from her left nostril, six from her right.

And they were long. I mean long. Each tentacle of hair was roughly seven feet in length. Bogeys and slime-like snot were dotted around the tentacles, making the sight more unpleasant than ever. Even Frederick, Aria and William leaned away from Gurt in disgust. One of the tentacles darted towards me. I slashed at it.

Somehow my blade simply slipped off the hair. I rolled backwards away from the attack from Gurt. I looked towards Chorus. The blade was covered in mucus. Green, gooey mucus. "Ewwww," said Chorus in a voice that seemed like it was trying all it could not to throw up, which made no sense as Chorus had no mouth or stomach.

Me pondering this didn't notice when another tentacle was arcing its way towards me. I saw it too soon. It wrapped around my legs, pulling them together. It then pulled me off my feet and threw me around. Eventually, the tentacle released me, sending me flying towards the side wall of the room. I passed the pillars and slammed straight into the golden wall. White lights danced in my head.

When I pulled myself back to my senses, I saw a tentacle flying, point first, directly at me. I had just enough time to roll away from the hair. Somehow Gurt's nose hair was capable of extending over ten metres, as Gurt herself hadn't stepped from the place she was standing a single bit since the assault began. My legs felt uncomfortable and sticky. I looked down to see thick snot stuck to my jeans, probably from the tentacles holding onto my legs.

I made a sharp turn, leaving the space between the pillars and the wall to the space in between both pillars, the space that had the carpet on. Looking towards the podium where the witches, Governor Frederick and the robed being were standing, I saw my four friends fighting off multiple nose tentacles each. Libbie's war-hammer and the other three swords were covered in the same snot Chorus was covered in.

They were also covered head to toe in the mucus. Two, three, even four tentacles some of my friends were fighting off. I then began to feel my Rimoor breakfast climbing back up my throat. "Pull yourself together!" I muttered to myself. I then noticed a nose hair tentacle just waiting in front of me. My guess was that it had reached its length limit and was waiting for me to step into its range.

But the creepy thing was that the length limit was an inch from my face. "Chorus, can we burn these things?" I asked.

"No, the mucus on them makes the hair flameproof," It replied. I then slashed at the nose hair, hoping that I would find a weak spot. In layman's terms, I did not. Instead, the tentacle wrapped around Chorus and tried to yank it out of my hands. However, with my heightened strength, I kept hold of Chorus.

But then the strength of the tentacle meant that I went flying across the room. The next thing I know, I am lying face flat on the carpeted floor, right in front of the steps up to the podium. I lifted my head. A warm feeling bestowed itself upon my upper lip. I reached up and felt my nose and lip and when I pulled my hand away, I saw blood stained across my fingertips.

I turned around suddenly, sweeping Chorus in a wide arc around me. With the momentum and strength of the swing, a hair tentacle that was heading towards my back was cut to the ground. I looked towards the rest of the hair tentacle. It then split apart into hundreds of tiny nose hairs, which all swirled around me, occasionally lashing out, and with the power and amount of the hair, I could feel the nose hair piercing my skin, ever so slightly drawing blood.

I twirled around so much, swinging Chorus around, but the sheer amount of the hair was overwhelming. I lifted Chorus up, pointing the tip to the roof, then a large sonic pulse emitted from Chorus, which immobilised the hair around me. It simply all dropped to the floor. I could now see the room around me again, my friends were still combating the tentacles. It seemed that only the hair that was assaulting me was the one that was knocked unconscious.

I spun around to face Gurt. I then ran up the podium and cut at her head. Unfortunately, since Gurt was twice the size of a fully grown adult, I only reached her chest. A fierce anger danced in Gurt's eyes as I looked up into them. I jumped up, willing Chorus to help me jump higher. Again I slashed. Even with the boost I only reached her nose. Seeking the advantage of the moment, I cut at some of the nose hair produced from her flared nostrils. Then the hair was cut.

Entire tentacles were cut out of her nose, them all slowly dropping to the floor. Gurt then raised her left arm and hit me, square in the chest. I was again flung all the way across the room. Once I rose, I looked towards my friends. They were all still covered in mucus, but they were only fighting one tentacle each now. It seemed that Gurt's nose hairs were most vulnerable at the exit points.

At that moment, I was also covered from my hair to the brim of my boots in snot. "Make your move!" Frederick, the Vicious, mocked. Somehow I was beginning to struggle to move. I looked down at my body. It seemed that the snot was crystallising into a solid shell of bogeys. I pushed myself forward again. After pushing at the shell, I had broken my way out of it, leaving shards of crystal snot on the floor.

"My floor!" The governor roared in anger. I again looked towards my friends. The snot on them was beginning to crystallise. I pointed my sword at them. The shell suddenly shattered off their bodies. Jim was then knocked straight off his feet by a tentacle. He hit the pillar, slid down it and didn't get back up.

I darted off, swerving and sweeping my way through the occasional bolts of crystal snot that the nose hair tentacles were capable of forming and flinging whenever and wherever they pleased. Once I reached Jim, I knelt down and checked his pulse. I could feel a heartbeat. "Oh lord," I whispered in relief. Jim was alive. I then snapped myself back to reality.

I was in the middle of a fight. I stood and turned towards the hairs. I ran back towards Gurt. I magically enhanced my jump as I jumped towards her. I then cut down the rest of the tentacles. I then turned around and ran down the stairs to my friend's side. Once I returned my gaze towards the beings on the podium, I could see Gurt looking puzzled and the others (except for the robed one) looking mortified at the quarter-giantess' failure.

"How!" William eventually shouted.

"A bit of skill," I replied. After I had answered William's question, Gurt's face then turned into a look of absolute fury. She let out an almighty roar. An enormous, double-sided war axe appeared in Gurt's grip. It was roughly twice the size of the regular war axe, the handle of it being made of wood and the blade of a rough metal. She held it in her right hand alone. The weapon had somehow materialised out of thin air.

Aria then raised her hands, a magical rune circle appearing in each of her palms. They were coloured a deep crimson, like the colour of blood. William then began to

179

levitate. He crossed his legs in mid-air, as if beginning to meditate. I prepared myself for a very dangerous fight. Gurt then jumped straight off the podium, bringing down her axe as she went.

I rolled away sideways. Her axe slammed ferociously into the ground, the blade digging into the marble floor.

"Hey! Watch the floor!" The governor shouted. Gurt turned her head towards me. I could tell she specifically was targeting me for cutting off her nose hairs. Aria then ran down the stairs, firing bolts of concentrated energy at my companions. All of the other three (as Jim was still unconscious) dodged the attacks.

Gurt stomped towards me, with no impatience on slaughtering me. She hefted her axe onto her shoulder. She then spun around really quickly. Someone her weight and size shouldn't have been able to do it, yet she somehow defied those odds and did it. Mid-spin, she removed her axe from her shoulder, pointing it out to her side.

Once she faced me again, she threw her axe at me. It spun at me like a boomerang, twirling around in circles. I narrowly missed it. It was so close that I was sure that it cut off some of my grey hair. Then, once it passed me, I turned to see it stop in mid-air, then move in the opposite direction that it was originally spinning and head back the way it came.

My eyesight followed the axe. Gurt then held her hand out and caught the weapon. Unexpectedly, as soon as she caught it, she lunged forward, sweeping her axe in a sideways motion. Like before, I narrowly missed the attack. I became certain that Gurt had been practising hand to hand combat much longer than she had been practising magic. I ended up not opposing her at all, instead I was just parrying and dodging all of her thrashes.

I realised that I could not beat Gurt all by myself. I sidestepped out of one of Gurt's downward assaults. Once I did this, I broke into a run around Gurt and to my friends. I saw her lumbering around to face me again. Her fierceness in her eyes did not waver. I turned my focus onto Aria. I believed that energy spells would be easier to beat than magical giantess brute force.

I began to walk towards Aria, who had then stood still, constantly firing blasts our way. Every energy blast she fired, Chorus absorbed as it deflected them. I could hear the booming sound of Gurt's feet as she dawdled towards me or my friends. But it did not steal my attention, my thoughts stayed stuck on beating Aria. The expression of fear spread across Aria's face as I came ever so closer to her.

Three metres. Two metres. One metre. Once I reached her, I...I... (sorry about this, it just makes me wonder where I will be going once I die) I cut off her hands. They dropped to the floor with a thud, the magical rune circles disappearing into thin air. Her wrists then sealed the wound. At the end of each arm, she had a bloody stub. Aria wailed in pain.

I heard Gurt's heavy footsteps stop in their tracks. I saw William turn his head towards Aria. She continued to scream in terror.

"WHAT HAVE YOU DONE!" She shrieked.

My own brain was asking me that exact question. What *had* I done? I wanted to give the witches a chance to recover from the enslavement, to save themselves. I didn't want to do *that!* I noticed Governor Frederick's jaw dropping. Aria then dropped to the floor. I noticed my blade was dug deep into her gut. I knew I hadn't done that.

William roared in anguish. "You killed my wife!" He yelled. "You killed her, I'll kill you!" A large blast of pink lightning emitted from nowhere, it was directed at me. I aimed Chorus' point at the lightning. My sword then, like it did Aria's energy blasts, absorbed the lightning. I had absolutely no clue that Aria was William's wife.

Then multiple events occurred at once. An earthquake happened, seemingly only at my feet, and a thunderstorm brewed right above me and my friends. The magic disasters shook me deep to my core. I was thrown everywhere because of the earthquake, and the storm produced loud lightning that always almost struck me.

I pulled myself together, stood up, and charged at William. He was only just levitating at human height, so I had a great shot at ending him.

"I'm sorry!" I shouted over the thunder. I then cut off William's head. His body and head dropped to the floor. The earthquake and the storm ended. As I was on the podium, I turned to face Frederick who was still on his throne. He had a ghastly expression on his face.

Abruptly, Gurt ran up the steps of the podium, grabbed me, and threw me off the heightened flooring. I landed face down on the carpet. My friends gathered around me, helping me up.

"Did you mean to kill Aria?" Austin asked.

"No, I guess it was a natural instinct," I replied. I then turned around and faced the podium again. Gurt was facing me with absolute, pure anger. She then summoned an enormous javelin in her free hand. She was dual wielding a war axe and javelin, both of twice the regular size. She stepped down the podium steps, not taking her eyes off me.

"Arrrgh!" She shouted before throwing her javelin at me. I sidestepped away from the javelin. It then pierced the ground where I had exactly been standing. It then removed itself from the floor and zoomed back into Gurt's hand. AHHHH! SCARY GIANT WITCH MAGIC! AHHHH! Gurt then lunged forwards, slamming down her axe.

Libbie *just* dodged it. Just afterwards, she jabbed with her javelin. Austin then jumped backwards, stopping the javelin from piercing his heart. The witch then crossed her arms, but while crossing, she threw both of her weapons. The javelin whistled through the air towards Libbie while her war axe circled its way towards Becky.

While this happened, I took the chance to attack Gurt. I stepped forwards, jabbing Chorus at Gurt's lower stomach, as that was the highest place I could reach without jumping. Gurt then savagely uncrossed her arms, swatting Chorus aside. With the power of the swat, my arm nearly snapped out of its socket. Blinding pain embodied me. I used my left hand to grab my right shoulder.

I could feel my arm only just hanging into my shoulder socket. As Gurt's weapons were flying back towards her, I ran to my right to stop myself being decapitated by the axe. I then tried to swing Chorus in the air to make sure that I was still capable of fighting. Instead of it being a strong, threatening strike, it was a weak, feeble slash.

"Ickle bickle magic boy too weak to fight the ugly witch!" Frederick taunted. Gurt then turned her head away from my allies and towards Governor Frederick, glaring at him. He then gulped very deeply. Gurt then roared out in pain. Still gripping my shoulder, I turned around to see Libbie withdrawing away from Gurt. I realised that while Gurt was distracted, she had slammed Gurt's leg with her war axe.

I almost laughed out loud. Almost. I used magic to relocate my arm. I felt it partially reconnect. "Why ain't it fully connected?" I demanded of Chorus.

"I suppose that magic cannot fix certain things," Chorus replied.

I then faced Gurt. I charged towards her, arcing my sword through the air as I ran. Now when I slashed, I felt less pain flaring through me. I successfully cut Gurt's hip. Without yelling, Gurt turned towards me. She used her javelin's pole to hit me aside. Instead of being smacked by the weapon, I used Chorus to soften the strike.

I simply stumbled backwards a few steps. Gurt stared at me, absently flinging her axe around to keep my friends away. She pushed her javelin harder but I was prepared. I pulled magic from Chorus and began to step forward. Soon enough, Gurt had the face of desperation, trying to stop me from approaching her, but I would not give in.

I used my smaller blade to my advantage. I suddenly ducked down and removed all strength on the javelin. The weapon soared above me, with so much momentum that there was no stopping it. I rose quickly and stabbed Gurt in her side. She bellowed again in pain. She dropped her javelin, gripped my hand which was resting on my sword hilt, and yanked out the blade. She swung her axe again.

I dodged and attacked, following this pattern for a while, my friends doing the same. After a while, we eventually tired Gurt out enough to beat her. She then summoned twenty daggers, all of them levitating behind her. The points were pointing in all directions that were away from Gurt. Suddenly, they flew outwards. I cut two of them out of the air and dodged the rest that were heading towards me.

My companions were also alright. She chucked her javelin to the floor and began to spin her war axe around. It was all that I could do to dodge the slices. My friends ran away from the slices, a more mature move than what I did. Instead, I charged at Gurt. I then jumped at her chest and put all my power behind one jab.

While I felt ferocious slashes tearing my flesh, Chorus dug straight into her chest. A single dribble of blood trickled down Gurt's robes. She stopped swinging her axe and dropped it. She fell backwards with a heavy slam. I removed Chorus from her chest. I then stepped backwards, my friends running up towards me. I felt incredibly lightheaded.

I looked at my clothes and saw excessive blood covering me. Large gashes passed through the clothes, passed through the flesh, all the way up to the bone. Gurt's chest then began to heave. She was breathing. She stood up and looked around hurriedly. Locking her eyesight on one of the large windows, Gurt jumped straight over me and my allies and ran at the wall.

She then jumped right through the glass window, into the snow. I looked back to Frederick, the Vicious.

"How's that for some kids!" I said to the governor.

"Oh Rince…" he muttered.

"You plead to the goddess who you abandoned. She will not answer your prayers!" Chorus shouted. Frederick dropped his head in shame. Or what I at least thought was shame. He then rocketed off his throne. He unsheathed his weird fencing-war sword and charged down the steps at me. I felt even more tired out. Too much blood loss.

A feeling of freedom circled through my veins as I grew more awake. Magic was healing my wounds. When Governor Frederick reached us, I tackled him with a heavy cut. Even though Frederick seemed like someone who could not do any damage himself, someone who acted behind others, he was surprisingly skilled with a sword. The handguard of the blade deflected my slash in the opposite way it was heading.

He then began slashing around, trying to catch me off guard. Many times he almost did. He was spinning around in 360 degree circles, with his blade outstretched, creating a whirlwind of threats.

"Stay back!" I called to the others. Frederick pushed me backwards more and more. He then rolled sideways, rising more quickly than what I would have thought possible in his armour. He continued his steady assault. His attacks were smooth but dangerous, clean but destructive. They were also ever so efficient.

He knocked my sword back but I retaliated with a downward strike. Frederick, the Vicious, pulled his sword away and stopped the blade in its tracks with his wrist armour. An echoing hum produced itself from the contact of the metals. I could feel a strong vibration through Chorus. Frederick's armour was somehow made of a metal that was of equal strength to Chorus' material.

Frederick then body-slammed me, sending me backwards. I could feel a variety of bruises forming all around my body. "Ugh. This guy is something else…" I mumbled.

"He is a governor for the Exelon empire," Chorus replied as Frederick marched towards me.

"I thought that meant they were meant to be wimps."

"Oh, Governor Frederick is the only governor selected for being one of the strongest living beings in the Exelon military. It's not just connectioooonnnnssss!" Chorus trailed off at the last word because I had quickly brung Chorus upwards to block a slash from the governor. He let out a gluttonous laugh. It was awfully joyous for the scene he was in. I pushed the sword away and climbed back to my feet.

We began to circle each other, swords at the ready. I was gripping my sword with both hands while Frederick was holding his weird sword in one. He seemed quite calm and active, going against the heavy, tiring blows he was dealing. "You seem awfully disturbed. You have never actively fought someone like me then I suppose." Governor Frederick laughed.

Absolute demon anger was boiling beneath my skin. I launched myself forward. I slashed and jabbed many murderous strikes but Frederick easily parried all of them.

"Why do you think the peasants call me Frederick, the Vicious?" The governor further mocked. I could hardly breathe, never mind talking. Wait what! I was struggling to breathe because my asthma was kicking in! I gasped. I noticed my friends' eyes widening in realisation.

"What are you doing? Wussing out?" Frederick asked. I began to stumble around, nearly collapsing to the floor.

"He's gonna die!" Becky cried out.

"Excuse me!" Frederick laughed. "He is dying!" He then burst out in laughter. He turned around to face my friends. He then walked away from me, towards them, his sword prepared for combat. I then drifted off to sleep.

187

Chapter 22

Asthma sucks. All I can say. Chorus must have controlled my breathing or I subconsciously went through my breathing exercises, but the next thing I knew I was waking up. As I opened my eyes, I saw Frederick beating all of my three conscious friends. Jim was still knocked out.

"OH GOD!" I shouted. I hurriedly stood, preparing Chorus with both hands. Frederick, the Vicious, then turned around, smiling uncontrollably. Even with his back turned, he was still beating my friends. I ran towards him, sword tip pointing at the governor's gut. Frederick then spun around, knocking all of my friends' weapons away.

Once he was facing me again, he outstretched his hands to his side. My sword then connected with the golden armour. Another loud ding echoed from the metals colliding. My sword slid off the armour. Frederick then hit me away. "Awake finally. Didn't take you long," said the governor humouredly.

I rose yet again from the ground. All of my companions charged Frederick on all sides. I charged again at his chest. Governor Frederick then ran forward, towards me. I sidestepped from his direction. Just before he passed where I was standing, he stretched out his sword and slid. The blade then grazed my chest.

"You truly are unskilled in the ways of combat, I haven't even broken a sweat yet," said Frederick, the Vicious. "And even if you were better, I would still beat you!" Blood then splattered everywhere. Frederick's head then fell down, cut clean off his neck. Becky stepped back, sword covered in blood. The body fell to the floor with a loud ding.

A cold, croaky laughter reached my ears. I turned around to look at the robed being. He was still in the same location. He didn't move at all. Then his head moved. The face of the hood turned towards me and my friends. Shadows still hid the beings face.

"Thank you," said the being.

"Who are you?" I asked with a shiver.

"I am death," replied the being.

"But I thought Lord Sulleth was the god of death," I countered.

"Well, he is the god, I am the embodiment."

"What are you doing here?" Libbie asked.

"I have been awaiting the moment that Governor Frederick dies. He took an extreme dislike towards me when he killed his cousin."

"That makes no sense."

"He said to me that I should have revived him. The concept of death is very complicated. You see, when someone dies, I take them to the Place of Stars, the afterlife. But Sulleth, he is the god, it means that he does not escort the dead, he can simply use death and control it."

"I would have thought that Rince escorted the dead to the afterlife, or at least she had some connection to death," Libbie said.

"Oh, she does. When living beings were first created, whenever one died, she used magic to automatically bring them to the Place of Stars, but that changed one day. Once, a millennia ago, the war of cultures began. Men of all kingdoms all turned into savages. It was only men as the royalty of that time were highly against female strength."

"Once the war ended, so many had died, in fact Rince was so disgusted at the death count, she created me, the embodiment of death. She claimed that the surviving savage men would have to now be taken by me to the Place of Stars, where they would live forever in a peaceful state, while all kindly beings, mainly women and peaceful men, would receive eternal paradise when she took them to the Place of Stars."

"It highly confused me what Rince did to punish the savage men before they died of age or disease, but that is for another time. I must now take my leave. I shall make sure Frederick receives much negative treatment in the afterlife," Death said.

"Wait, if there is a good afterlife, is there a bad one?" I asked.

"Oh, there is, but even Frederick hasn't disgusted Rince enough to take him there."

The being then vapourised, disappearing into thin air.

"W-what just happened?" Austin asked.

"I really don't know," I replied.

A large bang then reverberated around the room as the doors were knocked off their hinges. My eyes followed the sound, only to see multiple zombie warriors and golem warriors marching into the room.

"Damn, there's more," Becky muttered.

I hurried over to Jim's unconscious body. Kneeling down, I then sent a shockwave of energy into his body, knocking him awake.

"Ahgg! Nose hair!" he shouted. He looked around frantically to see a completely different scene, no tentacles, no witches, only the warriors walking ever closer onwards us. "Was I knocked out?" Jim then asked.

"Yes," I replied.

"Of course I did," he muttered.

We then rose up and began to walk towards the enemies. One of the golem's enormous swords were then brought down in a dangerous strike. The zombies unsheathed their weapons and ran towards us, the golems stomping slowly at me and my companions. It was a blur of combat. I was slithering between the forces, stabbing them with my newly ablaze blade. Many of the zombies fell to the ground, their rusty armour shattering apart as they hit the floor.

However, the golem warriors were resistant to most strikes. I had to find a crease in the golems plating to stab my blade in, always hoping to hit a vital component of the golems. Some of the golems blew up from the inside out, some of them had their hatch blown open, the slaves crawling away. But most of the time, the machines did not do anything, they simply continued their assault.

After what seemed like minutes, I had slayed all of the undead soldiers, me and my friends all having destroyed the robotic mechs or freed the slaves within them.

"We gotta get going!" I shouted to the others, over the groan of the final golem warrior toppling over. We then left the room and sneaked our way through Chalin fortress. We saw many zombies running through the hallways. The ones that actually came across us though, I quickly put them out of commission. "Where is the exit?" I demanded of a zombie warrior, my blade hilt deep in its gut.

It simply laughed and died again. It still annoyed me how something dead could die again, it was the wording that frustrated me. I removed my blade, cleaning the rust particles that were on my hands by wiping them on my winter travel coat. Of course, the mucus was still dripping on all of us, even though it was in small amounts, it was very irritating.

"Where are they!" I heard a zombie shout. I quickly turned a corner, beheading it as it came running towards the junction of corridors.

"Here we are!" I shouted at it frustratedly. I began to storm down the corridor, slaying all zombie warriors in sight. My friends were close behind me, simply cutting the zombies, only for them to reform, leading to me having to slay even more than I actively had to. I began to break into a run. I jogged down the stairs, my friends close in tow, running through the hallways.

I saw a zombie warrior at one point but I didn't want to stop the run, so I simply stuck my sword arm out. My sword chopped the undead in half, separated at the waist. Anxiety embodied me as I struggled to find an exit. Was I travelling in circles? Was I travelling deeper into the fortress? Those exact thoughts entered my mind.

I felt more secure knowing my friends were at my side. We then entered an area I wish we hadn't. It was the central atrium. It was enormous, with many elegant stairways leading all the way to the top floor. It was carpeted with a large rug of beautiful design. The roof of the atrium was domed, with a huge crystal chandelier hanging from the centre of the dome.

Statues were everywhere, mainly statues of Frederick and Vex. Oh, of course, there were loads of zombie warriors. Most of them were wearing the classical rusty armour with the worn out weapons, but there were still many warriors with polished, brand new weapons and armour. There were higher rank zombies than I had ever seen before.

There were also some living humans patrolling the room. Somehow we weren't seen.

"Guys, come," I whispered to the others. I began to walk through the atrium, marching in a way that made others think that I was meant to be there. However, some heads were still turned at the sight of us.

"Excuse me," said a well-spoken woman, stepping in front of us.

"Yes," I replied politely, holding all of my true emotions back.

"Where is your armour?" The woman demanded of us.

"Oh, forgot to put it on." I laughed dryly.

"And your weapons are very unnatural for the empire. You four wield harpes and a war-hammer, and you wield a golden sword, which the empire has never used," the woman urged.

"Errrm, exchange soldiers from the Capital Land," I replied.

"Wait, I remember you, your descriptions were given to us by Governor Frederick!" The woman snapped. "Intruders!

Enemies of the empire! Get them!" The woman suddenly shouted out.

It then became a slaughterhouse. A literal slaughterhouse. Blood was puddling everywhere, bodies falling to the ground. Some of the goriest deaths had occurred. So gory that I will not attempt to tell you how, for if I did, it will scar your mind. Enemies were charging down the stairs, only to be killed moments later.

Within minutes, every enemy in the atrium had died. I stood over the last one I had killed, breathing heavily. Now I wasn't just covered in runny mucus, but also in blood. In fact, some of the mucus had become stained red from the blood.

"We gotta keep on going," said Jim.

"Alright, just wait a moment," I said, willing Chorus to remove the disgustingness from me and my allies' bodies. All of the snot and blood then mixed together into a slimy clump of sickness, which then dropped to the floor. In front of me and my friends now laid a large clump of bloody mucus. I then stepped around it and began moving towards an exit on the opposite side of the room.

I was doing all I could to hold back the revolution. I then heard behind me the sound of throwing up. I decided not to turn back, for if I did, I was sure the revolt would come up. Once I reached the doorway that left the atrium, I heard my friends' feet pattering their way towards me. We then walked through the many corridors, trying to find an exit.

After what seemed like an hour, I finally saw it. I saw an archway that led into the open air. It was the first time I had ever felt truly relieved to see the open wilderness of Rimoor. I ran out of Chalin fortress. I felt the sudden harassment of the blizzard pounding against my skin.

I regret now not going around the fortress but I will never know if taking the extra time to do that would have led to as much death. But the horrors of the northern travels did not end there.

Chapter 23

I heard the shouts of the undead as I began to walk away from the fortress.

"Run north!" I shouted to my friends. As they ran past me, I spun around to face the zombies which were running at me. I hefted Chorus, the tip pointing at the warriors. A sudden pulse of energy emitted from the blade. It viciously hit the warriors, tearing the flesh from one of the zombies' bodies. As three fell to the snow, the remaining five charged at me.

I kept Chorus extinguished. Once one of the zombies reached me, I jabbed Chorus into its gut. The zombie laughed. Chorus then was set alight while inside of the undead soldier. The laugh was cut short, the laugh transforming smoothly into a scream. I removed Chorus and charged at the others. I cut one of them in half and beheaded another.

I then spun around, cutting the two remaining zombie warriors down. Arrows rained down from the windows of the fortress, zombies poking their heads and bows out. Most of the arrows missed. I turned tails from Chalin fortress and ran north. Then one arrow struck my shoulder. A bright pain seared through my head. I noticed the amount of arrows reaching me were lowering.

I turned back to see the last remnants of the fortress disappearing into the snow. Suddenly, an arrow zoomed out of the gloom. I then cut the last arrow out of the air. I returned Chorus to its bracelet form as to allow me to run quicker. While running, I reached up with my hand and pulled out the arrow that was stuck within my shoulder. I looked down at the blood covered tip.

I wiped the blood off the arrow head, to see if the tip was rusted or poisoned. Luckily, the tip was not rusted but was a regular arrow. No rust diseases today! Yay! Eventually, I saw my four friends standing around, waiting for me. I slowed to a halt in front of them. Their eyes automatically turned to the arrow in my hand. I dropped it.

"What happened?" Austin asked inquisitively.

"Well, I killed the zombies, then I ran. An arrow then hit me," I said simply.

Becky ran around the bac, to assess the wound.

"Alright, the wound is bleeding, quite strongly. But it seems that it is already healing. I can tell that your sword is helping you," she told me.

"Good," I said. Becky then walked back around to face me.

I panted, going through my breathing exercises. "I can't keep on doing this," I muttered. A hissing sound then occurred. I turned my head towards where the sound was emitting from. It was a hole in the ground that led down. Quicker than I could process, a load of water blasted out from the hole, which a millisecond later, froze.

It happened so fast in a way that made it look like an enormous spike of ice was flying out of the hole. "A frozen geyser forest…" Jim whispered. And it was. Oh it was. I could hear the same hissing occurring further north, all of the geysers hidden by the blizzard. I breathed deeply, listening to the hissing.

An ever so familiar laugh then echoed through the wilderness. Then something extremely large fell from the sky, landing right in front of us.

"Sssso you made it past Chalin fortresssss," Serpias mused. "I persssonaly thought you wouldn't make it thisss far."

"Damn," I mumbled under my breath.

"Now I will make you pay for dessstroying my little desssssert!" Serpias then rose up and slithered slowly towards us. At the same speed, me and my companions walked backwards. None of us had our weapons in hand. Serpias then flicked her wrists, her finger nails then elongating into talon-like claws. I could hear Jim gulping. I really didn't judge him.

"If you wish to apologissse for dessstroying my land, I will gladly take it."

"So you won't eat us?" Becky asked.

"Oh, who sssaid the apology let you live?" Serpias laughed. She then stopped slithering forward. We also stopped walking backwards. "It'sss just buisssnesss."

Serpias shrugged as she said it.

"We're screwed!" Austin said.

"We're definitely screwed!" Libbie said.

Serpias' claws elongated further. She then rose to near full height, using her tail to arch her backwards. The snake at the end of Serpias' tail hissed in a way that sounded like a laugh. She then quickly brung herself forwards, ending up slithering at maximum speed towards us.

We turned around haphazardly and ran north. Serpias chuckled coldly behind us. Soon enough, we reached the geysers. As we neared them, they began blasting up, as if sensing a living lifeform and deciding to make the chase even more dangerous. We weaved in and out of the geysers, which quickly shot ice spikes upwards.

The frozen geyser forest began to form around us as, in mass amounts, the ice spikes spawned. I turned around to see Serpias on me and my friends' tails. She had to slow down to weave through the frozen geysers. I turned back, narrowly missing a geyser spike. I dodged the ice spike by doing a fancy little side step.

The hissing that led up to the geysers erupting became quicker and higher pitched, signalling that the geysers' eruption speeds were quickening. Much fear streamed through me. More fear than I had ever felt before. I could hear the heavy slithering of Serpias as she snaked her way after us. More ice spikes blasted up around us, the hissing quickening so much that it was almost an instantaneous eruption.

I could feel sweat beading all across me, the sweat also beginning to freeze. Then, through the gloomy masses of the snow, the northern ice wall came into view. It was just as I imagined it to be. Tall, menacing, and so thick that you could not see through it. It was the same height as the western ice wall we had been following, but the northern version of it somehow seemed more opposing.

My attention swapped back to the frozen geyser forest as, yet again, I only just dodged an ice spike. As we drew ever so nearer to the ice wall, I dreaded what I knew to be me and my companions' fate. Finally, we reached the ice wall. I slammed my hands into it, beating it with my fists out of anger. Me and my friends turned around to face Serpias, who was beginning to slow.

I summoned Chorus while my friends unsheathed their harpes and Libbie unhooked her hammer. "Sssso, this isss how it ends for the so-called sssaviours of Rimoor!" Serpias laughed as she slowed to a walking pace. She slithered slowly towards us. "Thisss is the end of the line for you five," she mused. She was roughly six metres away.

Serpias then speeded up, arms reaching out towards us. Then an ice spike erupted from the snowy ground, coincidentally right below Serpias. The next thing I know, I was looking at an ice spike three metres away from me with Serpias' body parts scattered around it. Blood covered the tip of the spike. A few moments of silence followed.

"Is she dead?" Jim asked. I stared towards the disembodied head of Serpias, which was laying only a metre away. It was hard to believe, but she was.

"She's dead," I muttered. "She's dead!" I then shouted. I felt no remorse or sorrow for Serpias' death, only the emotion of joy. Even though blood stained the white ground, I felt unfazed. The tyranny of Serpias' chase was over! After a minute of celebration, we all calmed down enough to speak to one another in a serious way.

"We made it to the northern ice wall," Libbie breathed.

"Hard to believe we made it," replied Jim.

"I agree with what you're saying," Becky said. "It *is* hard to believe."

"But we did," I said. I looked south, thinking of how far we had travelled. I then turned my gaze towards my friends. Pride flowed within me.

"Now for the rest of this quest," Austin said.

Everyone turned south-east. Enormous mountains loomed many miles away, the peaks of some of the mountains being obscured from view. The colour of the enormous mounts were a deep shade of grey. "Well, this is gonna be fun!" I said. We then began to walk towards the Grey Mountains.

Printed in Great Britain
by Amazon

41025554R00116